The Lady

of the

Vineyard

a novel by

Kellyn Roth

Cover design by Cover Culture
Interior design by Wild Blue Wonder Press

Kellyn Roth, Author
Wild Blue Wonder Press
3680 Browns Creek Road
The Dalles, OR, 97058
www.kellynrothauthor.com

PRESS

For my dad, a profound influence on my life &
an amazing man of God.

"If you think this life is all there is ... then self-sacrifice must seem to you sheer insanity."

~*A Bird in the Tree* by Elizabeth Goudge

Table of Contents

Prologue

French Riviera
June 1938

Troy Kee whistled to his dog as he walked through the rows of grapes, occasionally stopping to check a vine. Holt barked at a cloud—or Troy assumed that was what he was barking at—his tail wagging and his yellow sides shaking, before frisking back to his master's side.

"Settle down, why don't you?" Yet Troy couldn't blame Holt. It was a beautiful day. Not too hot, not too cold, a slight breeze blowing up from the sea below, and the sun dancing down to dapple the ground between the grapevines.

The Lady of the Vineyard

Holt barked again before taking off to chase an invisible rabbit. Troy chuckled to himself. That dog had attention problems. He couldn't imagine what they'd do to him if he was a kid in school.

Satisfied that everything was as it should be, he turned back toward the house, calling to Holt again. Of course, Holt didn't listen, but Troy knew he'd catch up eventually—or at least when he remembered that his lunch came from his master.

At last, the odd little house, an English Victorian brick masterpiece combined with an Italian villa, came into view. Not a bit of France about it. Troy never would understand his dearly departed Uncle Henri.

The man had been a true eccentric.

Still, Troy liked his house. It looked grand with a fresh coat of white paint and dark green trim. It wasn't leaning, either, which was always a plus. He grinned. No Tower of Pisa here—at least not anymore.

If only … if only she'd come back to me. His heart did an odd little jump, surprised that he'd let his mind wander there. He never let himself think that way anymore; why had he done it? But the thought persisted: *If only I could share it with her.*

But she's not here, he reminded himself as gently as he could. He tried to be gentle with himself these days, as he knew too well the sting of harsh treatment. *She's not here, and you've got to have a life without her. It's the only way. If you kept on as you did the first few years, you'd kill yourself. You know that. So straighten up and smile.*

During his youth, he'd been so weak in his faith that it wasn't surprising he'd struggled as he had. In this world, where war once again brewed on the horizon, God was a necessity to any joyful life. But now, he was a God-fearing man, and a God-fearing man should possess at least some semblance of joy leading down the straight and narrow path to contentment and even a kind of happiness.

Troy reached the house and glanced over his shoulder to see Holt barrelling up the drive. He held the door open for the dog, then stepped through it himself.

Besides, if she came back, you couldn't let Holt in the house. That'd break his heart.

Troy had to grin a bit at that. Much as Holt meant to him, the lady's needs were to be considered over his own—or his dog's. She didn't like Holt's "particular smell." Though Troy had never noticed anything. To be fair, Troy's standards of cleanliness had never been woman-ized properly. He hadn't been married long enough, and his sister Lola, the only other woman he'd associated with beyond earlier childhood, was not one to complain about much of anything.

He walked through the house to the kitchen. Harrington, his friend, work partner, and former guardian, was sitting at the table, a newspaper in one hand and a mug full of coffee in the other. Troy went to the counter and poured himself a cup. That'd distract him from his mental wanderings.

He gestured at Harrington's reading material with his mug. "Anything good in the paper?"

"Um." Harrington snapped the paper in a way that spoke of *don't bother me; I'm reading*.

Troy smirked. He liked Harrington a lot—the man was a substitute father to him, after all—but he was always so grouchy. His constant prickliness meant that Troy seldom was able to take any small disgruntled noise seriously.

"No news, then? Same old, same old?" Troy scraped leftover scrambled eggs onto his plate, dropped it on the table, and forcibly removed Holt from his chair.

"Germany's restless."

"Germany's always restless." Troy took his seat and picked up his fork. "Anything new, I meant." A heavy cloud hung over Europe that hadn't quite been dispelled since the Great War, and even now Troy feared it was thickening. That said, he hoped for the best, even as he prepared—mentally and with foreign bank accounts—for the worst.

"It's getting more restless. But of course we can't be bothered to do anything about it, and frankly, I can see why, though I've never been one to ignore trouble brewing." Harrington made a disapproving growly noise at the back of his throat. He'd lost his dearest friend, Troy's uncle, in the Great War, and Troy guessed he wasn't too keen on the idea of another one.

For that matter, Troy wasn't, either. He tried not to think of it, but after losing his parents—truly, losing his entire way of life—to the war, the idea of entering another one didn't appeal to him at all. Yet he would fight, even as his father had done—and with less reluctance than his father, too. Where his father had seen needless bloodshed, Troy felt strongly that it was a man's duty to protect his country.

"They're skirting the issue." Uncharacteristically chatty, Harrington shook the pages out again. "You can read between the lines of any French paper now, though. It's all downhill from here ..."

Troy sighed. He was a realist, but sometimes Harrington's pessimism could get old. Actually, the first day Troy met him as a scrawny twelve-year-old kid who just wanted to move on and be happy, he'd already found it tiresome. Troy had so wanted to create a new life, a new family. *Too bad that is never going to happen.*

Harrington finished the article, neatly folded the newspaper, and set it on the table. He took another gulp of his coffee, glaring at Troy over the edge of the mug. "Troy."

He raised his eyebrows. Harrington was using his 'we need to talk' voice. "What?"

"Do you remember what day it is next week?"

Troy grinned. "Don't tell me I've forgotten your birthday again. Now, maybe if you told me the date, this wouldn't happen." Harrington didn't believe in celebrations over his ever-increasing age and so had declined informing Troy of the exact month and day when he became a year older. Some day Troy would figure it out, or at least, he'd harass Harrington until he was obligated to tell him.

"You know that's not it." Harrington fixed Troy with a grumpy glare. "I want to know if you're going to sulk off for the entirety of the day like every year like the lost soul you are."

Harrington was referring, of course, to a Most Important Birthday.

The birthday of a little girl in London who would be turning six next Saturday. Whom Troy hadn't seen in almost the entirety of those half a dozen years.

Yes, it always depressed him thinking of that little girl growing another year older without him, and he always spent the day tucked away somewhere where the temptation to snap and tear someone's head off was lessened. Still, he thought he might have more control over himself these days. He no longer drank—Drunk Troy was self-destructive, and he'd decided not to let the man out anymore—and he had a stronger relationship with God than ever before. Perhaps that would be enough to sustain him.

"I don't know what I'll do." Troy played with the eggs on his plate, stabbing them and then letting them slip off his fork. "A part of me thinks I can keep pretending. Pretend I'm not missing someone very important to me. But the other part ..." He sighed. "I

6

miss her, Harrington, and yet I can't be with her."

"Why not? That's your fault."

"It's not my fault that she … she left me." He growled at the back of his throat as he thought about it. It would have been a thousand more times easier to recover if he had been the one who ruined things, but he'd done his best and still she left him. Yet sometimes he wondered if that were true, for without God—and neither of them had had more than a passing acknowledgement of some kind of Mysterious Force—doing one's best would never be enough.

"That's wasn't the *she* I was talking about, and you know it." Harrington stood and dropped his coffee cup in the overflowing sink. Bacherlorhood suited them both well, but it wrecked the kitchen. "I'm talking about that baby you refuse to go see."

"She's not a baby anymore." Troy accidentally set his fork in his coffee then picked it up and regarded it suspiciously. He took a sip, including a bit of egg. *Just my luck*. He gagged and rose to dump the cup.

"Whatever. It's your fault you're too proud to see her. Your ex-wife made it clear the option is open. You're the one who has always separated yourself. Which I understood while you were a degenerate alcoholic—"

Troy grinned wryly. "Thanks."

"It's true, more or less. But now things have changed." Harrington shrugged. "Besides, if things really are destabilizing in Europe, you may be wasting

7

precious time, not to mention that everyone says that children grow up quickly."

Troy forced himself to smile. "Yes, well." He placed his plate in the sink. "I'll take that under advisement."

He left the room and walked up the stairs to his bedroom. It was a lonely walk. He let his shoulders hunch and his feet drag once he was out of Harrington's sight.

In his room, he shut the door and went to the bed. Sitting on the edge, he regarded the framed snapshot of a dark-eyed woman. She laughed merrily at him, impervious to his pain. Come to think of it, the real life lady wouldn't much care for his suffering, either—but she wouldn't laugh. At least, he believed she wouldn't laugh.

After a moment of staring at his beautiful lady, he opened the top drawer of the bedside table and pulled out a few snapshots, a bit blurry and crinkled, but distinguishable nonetheless.

A little baby, only a few days old, resting on this very bed with a chubby fist curled beside dimpled cheeks. He'd taken the pictures himself with a battered camera he'd barely known how to use. It was still in the attic, he thought, though probably not functional at this point.

They weren't good pictures, but the baby was fresh, new, innocent, and he loved her with every fiber of his being. The snapshots were about all that kept him going some days. They reminded him who he was working for, just in case the baby's mother chose to return to his side.

But, as he sat there, he realized the truth that'd been nipping at his mind for years, but which his pride and his weakness had always swept away.

He didn't need his lady to be a father.

Yes, his lady was a prerequisite to the original fatherhood situation. She'd made him a father. But it wasn't in her power to take that away from him. He'd always be a father in one way or another—had been since the moment God looked down at two weak mortals and decided to them went the responsibility of raising another soul.

But I can't be the baby's father again. Not without my lady. What was the point if she wasn't a part of the perfect picture?

Yet just because she didn't want and need him didn't mean that their child wouldn't.

"She's six now," he whispered, "or almost. More than a baby. A grown girl. I'm ... I'm missing her life."

It crashed down on his head then. Waiting for his lady's permission to reenter her life, to create a whole family, he'd lost his grip on what really mattered.

His daughter. The only person who truly belonged to him anymore. Except for Holt, of course, who wasn't quite human.

I don't know what tomorrow will bring. I probably won't ever win my lady back. But I can still be a dad. Oh, God, forgive me for waiting so long. Don't let it be too late.

Chapter One

June 24th, 1938
London, England

Judy perched on a low bench before a window overlooking the street. The lamplight outside caused her eyes to blink, and they stayed shut for longer every time.

It was past ten o'clock. She'd promised her mother she'd be in bed by nine, and that was even given the fact that it was her birthday eve.

However, Judy was not the kind of daughter who trusted her mother, light-headed as she could be, to arrive home safely after a date with her fiancé, Hal Acton. No, she had to stay awake; her mother needed her to wait up.

Nevertheless, the late hour was wearing. Judy rubbed her eyes, pinched her arm, and stood several times to shake all over like a golden retriever with an itch. None of this did much good, however.

Her pink bunny slippers stared up at her as if wondering why they hadn't been shoved under their owner's bed long ago. The clock ticked the minutes away angrily. It chimed the half-hour with much ado, urging her to hurry to her room and rest her head upon the pillow.

Time passed. Fifteen to eleven. Judy adjusted her dolly's gown and cradled her closer.

Marilou, a gift from Granny, was almost as big as Judy herself. She had blonde ringlets and blue eyes that clicked shut. The doll wore a dress that Judy's mother had sewn in the style of a low-cut, sparkly evening gown just to spite Granny. But Judy was proud of Marilou, despite the fact that Granny claimed she looked like a "cheap woman." Whatever that meant.

As the clock struck eleven, a taxicab disengaged itself from the regular flow of traffic and stopped in front of the building, its shiny black paint glowing in the streetlight.

Out jumped a short, broad-shouldered man. He turned and offered his hand to the other occupant of the back seat. She took it and stepped out.

Judy's mother wore a guardy turquoise dress made of a glittering, almost iridescent fabric, set here and there with glass beads. Standing at about five foot one, even her fiancé dwarfed her in size. She possessed flashing, obsidian-like eyes and self-curled hair of a slightly lighter hue. Her daughter thought she was the most beautiful woman in the world.

Yet now was not the time to stare. Judy leapt off the bench and raced around piles of dishes, books, papers, and other arbitrary items that lay about the living room. She hurried past the kitchen door, down the hall, and into the bedroom across from her mother's, Marilou bumpity-bumping behind her all the way.

In her bedroom, she carefully closed the door and weaved between various toys and clothes until she got to her bed. She heaved Marilou up onto it first, then rolled in herself. In a minute, they were both carefully tucked in. With her eyes shut, Judy held the peaceful look of an innocent baby angel on her rosy face.

Adele unlocked the door to her flat and turned the knob before glancing over her shoulder at her fiancé. "Can you come in, Hal? Have a cup of coffee, maybe?"

"I'd love to, but it's dreadfully late, isn't it?" Hal rolled his shoulders and glanced from side to side.

Adele had somewhat nosy neighbors who liked to comment on her dating habits, though to be fair, Hal was more to her than the other men. He was her latest version of forever.

Adele glanced at a diamond-set wristwatch, Hal's most recent gift to her. "Just after eleven."

"No, I guess I'd better not." Hal rubbed the back of his neck. "I've a busy day tomorrow. It's another of those golf lunches that I hate so much, and I've got to leave early in the morning and start north. You have that party, too, don't you?"

"Yes. And it's been a long day." Adele could already feel the softness of her pillow against her cheek, and she had to be up at a decent time tomorrow. It was Judy's birthday, and Mrs. Collier had some sort of event planned—at Adele's flat, no less. Adele's mother eternally had *something* planned which Adele didn't want to participate in.

Hal bent down and gave Adele a quick peck on the cheek. "Night, love. I'll be on my way."

Adele placed a hand at the nape of his neck and pulled him close for a kiss, relishing the touch even as she wondered how much longer she'd be able to make him wait. Then she released him and watched him walk down the hall.

She closed the door and kicked off her high-heeled shoes. They flew across the room and banged into a wall. She walked slowly to her room, dropping her hat and coat as she went.

I don't think I've ever been so happy since I was a kid, before all that stuff happened to me. And I'm doing the right thing if it makes me happy. I wouldn't be happy if I were doing the wrong thing ... would I?

She shook her head to rid herself of her dismal thoughts as she changed into one of her nightgowns. She *was* happy, and nothing else mattered. She was happy with Hal, happy with her job, happy with herself—and it had been a great deal of time since she was last happy with herself.

That was what mattered, wasn't it? Her own happiness. It was what this whole big empty world was searching for—happiness.

She must seek her own happiness, no matter the cost. Even if a few people, including herself, were hurt for a time as the happiness settled in.

Of course, I've got Judy to think about.

Even as the thought passed through her mind, the truth must be acknowledged. She didn't really like to think of herself as a mother. Or as twenty-nine, for that matter. Twenty-nine wasn't exactly old, but it was almost thirty, and thirty required a certain level of maturity that she wasn't quite willing to adopt.

She resolutely forced her lips to smile, lay down on her bed, pulled the covers over her head, and almost immediately fell asleep.

The Lady of the Vineyard

As the sun rose the next morning, Judy tossed back her covers and jumped to the floor. She managed to make her way out of her pajamas and into her best dress. She washed her face—somewhat carelessly—and combed her hair—not very thoroughly. Then she went to the kitchen and set about making tea and toast.

Her mother trudged out of her bedroom half an hour later. She yawned and ran a hand through her tangled hair. "How can you possibly be up at this incredibly early hour?"

Judy cocked her head. "We've got to start cleaning up for my birthday."

"Nobody's coming until three. We have all the time in the world."

Someone knocked at the door.

"I'll run and dress. You get that." Mother snatched up a cup of tea and a piece of toast as she hurried back to her bedroom.

Face set seriously, Judy walked slowly to the door, grasped the handle—which was slightly above her head—and strenuously opened it. As soon as the door was open, Judy's heart did a little jump of joy. "Granny!"

"Judy!" Granny knelt to hug her granddaughter, and Judy buried her face in her shoulder.

Judy didn't get a lot of affection outside of her Aunt Millie, who stopped by when she could, so she always snuggled in and held tight. Aunt Millie,

Mother's best friend since childhood, could always be counted on for a hug, but she was also rather busy.

Granny drew back and glanced about the room before her eyes returned to Judy's upturned face.

"Mother's just getting dressed," Judy said.

Granny looked Judy up and down then sighed and reached to smooth her hair. "I see you've dressed yourself."

"Yes."

Granny frowned. "She never does take time with you, does she? I took pride in seeing that my children looked pretty—but of course Adele doesn't care."

Judy smiled and placed a hand on her grandmother's cheek. "Don't put on your sad face. It's my birthday!"

Immediately, her expression brightened, and she gave Judy another squeeze. "Yes, so I've heard! Six years old, is it? Just the other day, I was holding my baby granddaughter in my arms and marveling at how tiny her fingers and toes were, and now look at you!"

Judy wiggled with delight. It was always good to hear that one was getting older. She wanted nothing more than to get good and old. Old people could do just about anything, things little girls couldn't. It must be lovely to be practically ancient and be able to go anywhere whenever one wanted to with no restrictions.

"Now, let's see what we can do to get you looking pretty for your party. Adele!" Granny rose and walked briskly through the living room. "Adele, what are you doing? Your daughter looks like a gypsy."

Mother's moan of frustration could be heard clearly from the bedroom. "In a moment. I'm only half-dressed. Do stop fussing! I wish you hadn't come so early."

Granny sighed and turned to the kitchen, mumbling under her breath. Judy followed quietly. There was another knock at the door, and she rushed to answer it.

"Aunt Millie!" Judy threw her arms around her honorary aunt's legs, almost knocking her to the ground.

"Hello, baby." Aunt Millie awkwardly dropped an armload of packages to the floor and gave her adopted niece a big hug. "I brought you some presents. That one, and the long box, you can open now, and those two are for later."

Judy forgot all about smothering Aunt Millie in affection and dropped to her bottom to begin opening the first package, which turned out to be roses from Mother and Aunt Millie's shop. The second was some cakes for the birthday party from a bakery down the street.

Aunt Millie repositioned her glasses, which had been knocked sideways due to Judy's hug. "Is Adele in her bedroom?"

"She's getting ready." As always, Judy wished that her mother would let her watch but didn't dare ask. She loved seeing Mother curl her hair and put on her

18

makeup and perfume. She loved watching her sort through her jewelry to find the perfect piece to compliment her frock. She loved watching her pin on her hat and slip on her heels and twirl before the mirror, admiring the final effect.

It always made Judy wish she could be a beautiful lady like her mother, putting on pretty things for a night on the town or a party.

Aunt Millie brushed past Judy and into Mother's bedroom, and Judy watched her go, fighting back the sadness.

Adele glanced at Millie in the mirror as she entered the room and closed the door behind her. She smiled and motioned her best friend over.

"There you are. What do you think of this new shade of lipstick? Too dull?"

Millie blinked, her glasses shifting slightly as her nose wrinkled. "Actually, I think it's bright."

Adele almost laughed. Millie always thought her lipstick was too bright, her jewelry too flashy, and her clothing too low or too high depending on the end. "Then it must be perfect." She winked and applied another layer of rouge. "Did you bring the flowers and the cakes?"

"I did. I wish you'd bought them and given them

to Judy, though." Millie's brow was wrinkled as she placed the receipts and change on Adele's vanity.

"Oh? Why?"

"Because Judy always thinks everything good comes from someone other than you, and it'd be nice for her to fully realize that you can bring something lovely into her world."

"I bought her a present." An entire box of doll clothes for Marilou was under her bed, in fact.

"I know, but I can guess the way you'll act when you give it to her. Casually, as if it doesn't matter, as if you regret the decision to get her something." Millie sighed. "There's no feeling in it, Adele. She's just a little girl, and she doesn't understand. She doesn't understand being scorned because her father wasn't able to live up to your standards. Furthermore, no one but you can give her love in the precise way she needs."

Adele moaned aloud. "Oh, for heaven's sake, Millie!" Again and again, these things were said, and again and again, Adele told Millie she didn't want to hear them. Judy was a sweet girl, but Adele knew better than to let her get too close. She couldn't help but like her daughter a little, as a sort of acquaintance, but loving and caring for her as her mother was too much to ask of a woman like Adele.

"I know, I know. I said I wouldn't lecture you anymore, but ..." Millie wrapped her arms around herself. "It's just that Judy is turning out a lot like Troy. She's sensitive in the same way—and yet she never forces herself on you. She won't show you that she cares about you unless you show her first. Troy was the same way. He was good for you, even if you never could let him reach into your heart. Don't you realize—"

Adele's chest tightened. "Millie. I thought we weren't going to discuss this." She couldn't talk about him. If she talked about him, she started to feel guilty, and if she started to feel guilty, she wouldn't be happy. She must keep control over her happiness.

"I know, I know. But sometimes, when I look at sweet little Judy and think about what you voluntarily gave up, when I have wanted nothing more than the life you tossed away—" Millie stopped herself then and went to the closet. "Do you have a cardigan I could borrow? It's a bit chillier than I expected for June, and I don't want to run back to my place." Millie lived in the small attic-converted-to-flat above the flower shop she co-managed with Adele.

Adele rose and went to help Millie find the right piece to match her dress from her veritable landslide of clothing items. She never picked up after herself, and she was always buying new clothes, so things got messy in a hurry. However, she did have a good idea where things were, usually.

Yet even as she helped Millie find a cute little jacket that brought out the blue in her eyes, she managed to finish Millie's sentiment: "It should have been me." Adele felt like that sometimes, too. That Millie was more deserving and suited to her ex-husband than Adele had been.

Troy Kee. She always shuddered a bit when she thought of him, so she tried not to. Conservative, calm, his actions and words and feelings set in stone by his darned ethics or religion or whatever he wanted to call it. Troy wanted to settle down and make her into a little housewife, wanted to raise a batch of brats with her, wanted to grow old with her in two rocking chairs by the window.

Troy was the perfect man, supposedly. Adele's mother adored him, and she'd never forgiven Adele for leaving him. Though Adele knew that, at least when they'd been married, there'd been something less than sincere about Troy's morals, and certainly he'd been foolish in some of his actions. Not that Adele had been anything more than a fool, but at least she was honest about it. Troy's hypocrisy bled into his every action, though he tried hard to rise above it. Millie felt his marriage to Adele was proof of that, which wasn't flattering, but she understood what her best friend meant.

She wondered vaguely if he ever had grown up. It was probable he had, but in doing so, he would have far outgrown her.

Which meant the restraint of his love would be even more felt now than it had been during their brief marriage.

Adele's mother didn't understand that she needed to be free. That her heart had strained being attached to one man for life. Though it wasn't that, after all. She was engaged to be married now, and she didn't think she'd tire of Hal Acton.

Hal was different than Troy. He didn't want children, he was content to send Judy to boarding school, and he was used to the careless, extravagant lifestyle she treasured. He wouldn't expect her to settle down. She needed that.

Perhaps she hadn't run so much from Troy as from the man she had known Troy would become, especially as a father, though hopefully he had managed some growth even without the extra push of a child. She hoped so. Though she didn't love him, she didn't wish him ill, exactly.

Yes, it should have been Millie who ended up with a nice man like Troy and had a sweet girl like Judy, for goodness knows Adele didn't know what to do with them. She loved Judy in the deepest part of her soul but was bad at expressing it. Troy, she couldn't love, at least not in the way he wanted and needed. Millie would have provided that love.

Unfortunately, no attraction existed between them. Rather a shame, though it was unlikely Millie would take one of Adele's castoffs anyway. She never had before. Of course, most of Adele's men hadn't been of nearly the same caliber as Troy Kee. Adele was always forced to admit that.

She didn't know what to do with a little girl, and besides, her own pleasure was a better pursuit in her opinion. Drinking, men, dancing the nights away—these made her happy, and it was easier to fall back in the pattern she'd inhabited before she married Troy than to form a new one.

Millie cleared her throat. "At least your mother seems to be more comfortable being at your flat than she has in past years. Before, she'd never have hosted a party for Judy's friends here—she'd just whisk Judy off to her home for a week and leave you out of the birthday completely. Is ... is your relationship getting better?"

Adele's mother, Mrs. Collier, had never gotten along with her only living child. Yet, when Adele left Troy and returned to London from France with baby Judy, her mother had sold her home in Kent and unhesitantly bought a house in London to be near her granddaughter. She'd done a lot of growing, too, to accommodate the affections and needs and desires of a small child. Now, she seemed to anticipate Judy's moods far quicker than Adele could.

Not that Judy was a particularly moody child. She could just be a bit difficult to read from time to time. Awfully quiet. Even now, she hadn't made any close friends—she'd started school in September, but the teachers had called her 'odd' and 'shy.' Yes, Judy spent time with children her grandmother introduced her to, in a polite and proper way that always led Adele to roll her eyes. She didn't like the teachers insulting Judy, of course, so she'd pulled her out for a few months and was considering starting her again in September—or sending her to a different school. She wasn't sure what.

Odd that Mother loves Judy so much when she failed to thrive at school. Any kind of 'stupidity' from Adele had not been tolerated throughout her childhood. Still, Adele's mother adored Judy. Strange as it might seem, the small child had given Mrs. Elizabeth Collier a surprising second life that even Adele couldn't ignore.

Her perfect daughter, Adele thought bitterly. *The replacement to her wicked child, who dates around and drinks and leaves her husband.*

"Oh, you know Mother. God is good, Adele is bad, and you can't serve two masters." She winked, but Millie frowned.

"Why isn't, um, Harry here?"

"Hal," Adele corrected. Millie didn't care for Hal Acton for whatever reason, and this time she wasn't hesitating to show it. However, Adele had chosen to ignore her best friend's negativity in that area. Millie was such a loyal friend in other ways, even though she disagreed with basically everything Adele did nowadays.

"Right. Why isn't *he* here?"

"Because he had a business meeting out of town. I told you that. He's a very important man of commerce, and he has a great deal of these kinds of social engagements." Which Adele would doubtless be required to participate in as his wife. Nothing could suit her more. The wife of a successful businessman, an up-and-coming wealthy man who would meet all sorts of important people and host all sorts of lavish parties for them, was much more to her taste than a chalet in France where she met no one, did nothing, and didn't even speak the same language as her neighbors anyway.

"Hmm. I don't listen to anything about him, and I freely admit that, cold as it might seem." Millie shrugged. "I don't do it on purpose. It just happens."

Adele smiled weakly. "Darling, I'm going to marry him whether you like it or not. We're planning an autumn wedding—a proper wedding this time, so I'll want you to be my maid of honor. So don't think you can convince me not to with your disapproval. You know I won't pay any attention."

Something like hurt appeared in Millie's eyes. Adele knew that expression well, though she did her best not to arouse it in her friend too often. "My opinions don't matter to you, I know. But sometimes I do speak common sense. If you weren't able to stay married to a man who was nearly perfect, Adele, how will things be different with this Hugo character?"

"Hal."

"Whatever."

"Hal's ... Hal's different." Adele sat on the edge of the bed and began rolling her stockings on. "Hal will give me the freedom *he* never could."

"Troy. Troy Kee. Your husband."

"Ex-husband."

Millie cocked her head. "I was never taught that a marriage could just end like that. I thought one or the other rather had to die."

Adele smirked. "That's old-fashioned, Millie."

"Well, then, I'm old-fashioned!"

"I know that." She touched up her powder one last time. "Come on. Let's make an appearance before Mother takes to burning photos of me."

The Lady of the Vineyard

Chapter Two

By the time Granny, Aunt Millie, and Judy finished cleaning the incredibly cluttered flat, it was past noon and soon Judy's "little friends," as Granny called them, would be arriving for the party.

In truth, Judy didn't know her "friends." They were all grandchildren of her granny's many church friends who Judy had only met a few times and didn't much care for. But she supposed that wasn't quite fair. She just didn't know them.

However, Granny wanted Judy to have friends, so Judy would try. She'd do anything to please Granny, after all. Who else in this world did she have to please who would actually notice?

Aunt Millie, she supposed, but Aunt Millie just wanted a hug every so often and some acknowledgement that she existed. Judy could do that. After all, wasn't that what she wanted, too?

Granny set about preparing the refreshments only to find a disturbing lack of the correct ingredients. So she gave Judy a list and told her to run across the street to the grocery and give it to Mr. Tilney along with a little purse containing the sum that would be required to make the purchases.

As Judy exited the flat building, she noticed a tall, skinny man sitting on the curb, wearing a rumpled business suit. He had removed his hat and was twirling it around and around on his finger. His reddish hair was messy and his blue eyes distant. He had a small mustache on his upper lip—at least it was neatly clipped, though. A mustache was bad enough, but a messy mustache was unbearable in Judy's opinion.

Judy tilted her head to the side, took a step nearer the man, and tried to see what he was staring at across the street.

She could see nothing worth such serious deliberation. Just Mr. Tilney's store and Mother's flower shop and the small flat over the flower shop.

The man seemed to be staring at nothing, into a distance that didn't really exist.

He turned. The two stared at each other for a few incredibly long seconds before he cleared his throat.

"Who are you?" His voice was strangled, and his eyes fastened on her face in a hungry sort of way.

She didn't know what to think of that. It didn't seem mean, but she'd been given so many warnings about mean men that she knew she ought to be cautious. "Judy." Surely telling him her name wouldn't hurt a thing.

"I know. At least, most of me knew." The man straightened his back and looked her up and down before returning to her face, a bashful grin twisting his lips.

"Then why did you ask?" asked Judy.

"Because I wanted to be sure." He ran a hand through his hair and watched her with eyes a bit closed, like he was wincing in pain. "Sometimes it's good to double check before assuming something, especially if you've gotten in trouble before for not being sure and assuming and moving too fast for your own good."

"Oh." That made sense, she supposed. Caution was definitely preferable. One didn't make mistakes if one were cautious, and mistakes weren't something her mother appreciated. Especially ones that caused a mess Mother had to clean up. Not that she ever cleaned unless she absolutely must. Mother didn't mind most messes. The cleaning up messes part, however? It made Mother most cross. Judy hated when her mother went from not caring at all to being cross. It was the worst feeling in the world.

"You look like your Aunt Lola," said the man,

31

referring to the paternal aunt who visited occasionally. "But your hair isn't curly like hers."

"I know," said Judy. "It's curlier when my braids aren't so tight." She tugged one to show how tight and unforgiving it was.

"Mine would curl if I let it grow, probably. Like my mother's hair." His voice was raspy, and Judy wondered if it was always like that or if he was just sad right then. "Who told you you look like her?"

"Aunt Lola," said Judy.

"Oh." He stood. Judy was obliged to crane her neck to continue looking him in the eye. He was quite tall, and not just because Judy was quite short. Her mother was half his size, she was sure. "Are you supposed to be talking to strangers?" the man asked.

Judy shook her head. "I'm *supposed* to be getting these things and hurrying back," she said, holding up the slip of paper.

He accepted the grocery list and gave it a looking over before passing it back to her. "Well, then you'd best be about your business."

"Will you be about your business, too?" Judy asked.

The man nodded, and his voice cleared a bit as he replied. "I will. I need to see my sister before I go to a party, or she'll be mad at me. We can't have that."

"Good. You looked lonely sitting on the street there."

"Did I?" The man had an odd little twist to his lips

32

now that told her he had some sort of feeling that wasn't quite comfortable.

Judy offered a bit of a smile to set him at ease. "Yes. And that's no good! After all, there are so many people in the world that one oughtn't to be lonely!"

Or at least one oughtn't to be lonely when one was a big man who could go anywhere and meet anyone. Judy couldn't really make friends because she got in trouble for wandering off, and it was hard enough making friends anyway, but the man could do anything he wanted. He could make dozens of friends. Judy felt a flash of jealousy but quickly reined it in.

The man laughed dryly. "Well, what if there was only one person in the world a fellow wanted to be with?"

"Then he'd better be with that person." Judy glanced across the street. "I'd better go. Granny will be worried. Besides, I guess you are a stranger, and Aunt Millie says you might be mean, even in places I think are safe. She's most afraid someone will be mean to me."

"Very well. Run along, Judy."

Judy paused. "How'd you know my name?" Strangers weren't supposed to know her name.

"You told me, baby," the man reminded her, eyes twinkling.

"Oh," said Judy. She stood still for a moment, contemplating whether strangers ought to call her "baby," then she hurried across the street and into Mr.

Tilney's store.

In no time at all, she was back out with the groceries. The man was gone.

~

Adele didn't think anyone could blame her for tucking herself away in her room when all Judy's "friends" came over.

Mother had invited about ten of them, a variety of boys and girls, and the room was crowded enough without her being in the way.

Besides, she didn't care for children. They were so small, so delicate, so easily startled and scared. They were also quite noisy. Adele didn't understand the ceaseless cacophony, nor could she easily bear it.

It also made her guilty.

Shouldn't she like children? Weren't women supposed to want and treasure babies? What was wrong with her? Why couldn't she experience a natural feeling in all her life? Yet she couldn't make herself feel in a way she didn't feel. That was impossible. It was better to simply distance herself from those below the age of sixteen for good.

It didn't help that, in Judy, Adele saw the reflection of a girl about her age, so many years ago. A girl who watched her mother crumple and cease to behave naturally during a war that took everything from them. A helpless little girl whose only hope was to look to an uncertain future for uncertain comfort.

No, she never wanted to think about that again.

Little girls brought the memories back in a rush, reminded her that they could feel the same agonizing pain and loneliness and confusion that she had.

That once upon a time, Adele Collier hadn't been a self-assured woman with an army of men at her feet but rather a frightened child whose own mother had abandoned her when the need for comfort was greatest.

No, it was best not to think about that. The memories were too painful. It was best to simply pretend she disliked children because she was a terrible person. Being terrible was easier than being broken.

Besides, Granny and Millie both loved Judy and children—they made better hosts. Another woman in the room would be unnecessary and quarrelsome.

So many reasons to make a polite exit from Judy's birthday party and let the festivities unroll without her.

Halfway through the party, there was a knock at the door. Judy went to answer it at her grandmother's urging. When she opened it, there stood the man from the curb. She blinked once, blinked twice, then a slow smile took over her face, forcing her cheeks up and bringing laughter bubbling to the surface.

Why, the party he'd been coming to must be hers!

The Lady of the Vineyard

"Hello! Did you come for my birthday?"

"Yes," said the man, equally as matter-of-fact. "I hope I'm welcome!"

"Of course you are." Judy held the door wide open. Anyone who was lonely was welcome as far as she was concerned. She saw a lot of herself in this strange man—and not just those blue eyes.

"Judy, who's that?" Granny came around the corner. She gawked at the sight of the man. "Why ... Troy!" Judy thought for a moment that her grandmother's jaw was going to hit the floor. "What are you—I mean, how did you get here?" Granny had that tone that said she was trying to be polite but struggling mightily with her shock.

Judy hoped Granny wouldn't make the lonely man leave.

"I walked up the stairs, down the hall, and knocked on the door." The man explained. "Della invited me."

"She ... did?" Granny raised her eyebrows. "Of course, we're glad to have you, Troy," she amended, "but I just didn't think Adele would—"

The man's face changed, his smile quirking a bit so it wasn't entirely natural. He reminded her of someone, though she couldn't think who. "*Naturellement*. Why invite the proud father? That's not like my Della at all. Granted, she didn't invite me to this party *exactly*. She said if I wanted to drop in and see Judy some time, I could, and she didn't fight for full

36

custody almost six years ago when she could have. We were to come to a private arrangement about visitation—we just never did. So I'm visiting now."

"I'm sure you're very welcome." Granny's tone was slightly nervous.

Judy gawked and took a step toward the man. She slid her fingers into his hand and tugged at them to make him look at her.

"Daddy?" It was a question, not a statement, for she wasn't quite sure yet. It couldn't be—and yet it must be. After all these years, why now? He couldn't like her much, if he'd never been there before. Yet here he was.

He smiled. "Judy's glad to see me, at least. Aren't you, baby?"

Eyes wide, Judy nodded.

At the sound of his voice, Adele jumped. She stood up from the chair where she had been sitting, buried in a novel, and went to the door to listen. She couldn't quite make out what was being said, but she *did* know that it was *him*.

Why was he here? In the past five and a half years, almost six come August, she hadn't heard a word from the man, besides the occasional letter that she returned unopened. She wasn't going to make contact easier for

Troy if he wasn't going to put the effort in. He was the one who had broken contact with Judy. She'd left the door open for him, or at least unlocked, and he'd never tried the handle.

Still, she'd thought he'd come—or at least send a lavish present—for his beloved Judy, for he had loved the child during those first early months. Troy liked giving lavish, ridiculous presents. He'd bought her a car once upon a time when they were more in love than anyone had a right to be.

That was a long time ago. Perhaps his buying habits had changed. Still, she knew Judy would've liked to hear from him—and Adele resented his absence as much as she resented his presence.

It was so unlike the Troy she'd known to abandon a baby girl for no discernable reason. People changed, of course. Even people like Troy, who'd always been as steady as the day was long.

Why come now, though?

She touched her hair lightly with her fingertips, inwardly cursed herself for her habitual primping, and walked into the living room.

There he sat on the best chair in her flat, bold as brass, chatting with Judy's party guests and flattering her mother and Millie shamelessly.

Judy was enthroned on his lap with a pearl necklace around her neck. A pearl necklace that Adele had never seen before. Now *that*, that was just like the old Troy, buying some ridiculously costly gift for such a little girl. Judy would probably lose it or ruin it. At least it was pearls and not something like diamonds.

"Troy," she said levelly.

His eyes immediately went to her face and gave her a quick once-over. There was an emotion, some of that desperation that he'd exhibited so often during the divorce proceedings, that flashed across his features before he quickly hid it, keeping his expression casually friendly, almost playful but not quite. "Della! Where have you been? You're missing all the fun." No introduction, no explanation, as if he sat there all the time. With *her* daughter.

Judy was Adele's now. Didn't he know that?

"What are you doing here?" The words came out even colder than she'd intended, snapping past her lips with an anger she'd thought she'd grown out of. Perhaps she hadn't. Perhaps it was an anger reserved for him.

He grinned and shifted Judy on his lap, his arm tossed about her baby girl, holding her close, like he had any right on earth after all those years away. "Oh, for heaven's sake, Della, don't make a scene!"

"Make a scene? I don't think I'm making a scene! I'm being perfectly reasonable. You show up at my flat after I haven't seen you—have barely heard from you— in almost half a dozen years, and *I'm* the one who's making a scene? Of course. Because it's all my fault. Because *I* left *you*," Adele huffed, folding her arms in front of her chest. She couldn't believe him. Of course he'd play the victim. Because she was the wicked unchristian heathen. She deserved it.

Adele hadn't been a victim since she was seven years old. She supposed she ought to be glad she'd obtained the reputation she'd strived for—that of the perpetrator and the villain.

"Though that *is* true, I don't think this is the time to discuss it," Troy said in a low voice. "Let's talk about it later."

Her heart clenched. Later? There would be no later. She'd removed his right to "later," same as "forever" and "tomorrow." But they must discuss this. "You're right. Why don't you come back later?"

"Adele." Granny put a restraining hand on her arm. "This is a bad time for you and Troy to quarrel over details. I won't have you ruining Judy's birthday party, and I won't have you disgracing me in front of my friends' grandchildren."

Adele relented but refused to stay in the same room with him. She whirled on her high-heeled shoes and marched back into her bedroom, where she tried to read.

She didn't succeed. After all, that detestable excuse for a human being was in her living room, and she could only think of ways to get him out of her flat and her life.

After the last of the guests left, Adele came out of her bedroom. Troy sat on the kitchen table, enjoying leftover birthday cake with Judy's help. He jumped up when she entered the room, then sank into a chair with a sheepish grin.

Good. He was far too tall to yell at when he stood.

Adele placed her hands on her hips, knowing she didn't cut a very impressive figure at her height and wanting to at least strike a dominant pose. "Why are you here?"

"I have every right to come see my daughter when I wish to. Even you wouldn't be so unreasonable as to keep her away from me." He shrugged. "In fact, I think there are a number of papers signed and agreements made that give me a right to at least a few weeks a year."

"Yes, but you've never shown the least interest in her until now. Why would you all of the sudden?" Something must have happened that made a reasonable man do such an about-turnaround.

Troy winced and glanced at Judy before returning his eyes to Adele's face. So that struck a chord, did it? "I was in London on business."

"Business?" What business did the owner of a French vineyard have in London?

"Yes. Business. Most of my money remains in England, although my unworthy carcass may not under usual circumstances, and I had a meeting with a banker about certain investments I made. Does that make sense, or must I explain my every action and decision to you?" His tone was carefully restrained, but there was a biting edge of sarcasm to it. So he was bitter.

She'd wondered at his calmness before.

Adele nodded. "I understand that you have business in London—and there's your sister, too, I guess. But why come to see us?" *After all this time. After you didn't seem to care about me—I mean about Judy, of course—anymore.*

His face hardened for a moment before he forced it back into calculated nonchalance. "Don't flatter yourself. I came to see Judy. I remembered it was her birthday and wanted to get a look at my daughter. After all, I thought she might have grown, and I was curious as to how you grew her—or if *you* did at all."

"You'll be going soon, though, I hope?" The way Judy looked at him with adoring eyes scared Adele. *What if I lose Judy? What if she wants Troy more?*

"Not until next week. I intend to spend as much time with Judy as I want before that not-so-distant date."

"Oh." The sooner he was out of her life, the better. After all, if he tried to be a father even a bit, her maternal insufficiencies would stand out even stronger. They were already so defined; he needn't highlight them. "You can't expect just to show up here whenever you please. From now on, if you want to see Judy, call first, and we'll arrange a time."

He grinned. "I find that a bit of a bother. I prefer impulsivity."

"If you want to see Judy, you won't mind the bother." Her smile felt tight.. *The liar. He couldn't be impulsive if he tried. He's just saying that. I'm the one who wants to be impulsive. He's set in stone, a boring old man.*

"Hmm. I suppose there's no chance of me sleeping here tonight?"

"Of course not!" Her tone was sharper than she'd even intended, but if he thought he could just waltz back in and resume things as normal, he should think again. "I don't care where you sleep as long as it's nowhere near me."

A chuckle burst from his lips. "That wasn't what I meant, Della; I meant on the sofa. But funny that your mind hopped there, isn't it? Careful. You'll make me think you missed me." He winked. "Very well. I'm sure my sister won't mind me occupying her living room." He stood and picked up his crumpled hat. "Oh, and I think I'd like to take Judy back with me for the summer."

Adele blinked. "What?"

"I want to take Judy back. With me. To France. For the summer." His smile broadened. "Your mother said she is out of school until September—how kind of you to consider her feelings, Della! Though I know it must've been so you didn't have to take her every morning as for her own good. I hear you're considering a different school, which I'd like to hear about. But for now, all that matters is it gives her a nice, long holiday to spend with me."

"You can't." Adele couldn't let that happen.

"That's not what we arranged."

His eyes caught hers, despite her best attempts to avoid his gaze. He made her want to shrink into nothing and die. Why was he so good at hiding his fears, which he must have, when she was at her most vulnerable? "What do you mean? That's exactly what we arranged, Della. I think the agreement was two months during the summer at the vineyard after she was three and visits permitted if I wanted them throughout the year. Or do we need to dig out those documents? I think I have them with me, actually." He extended a hand as if to pick up the briefcase he'd left sitting on the floor near him, but instead of actually taking action, he just smirked at her and straightened in his seat once more.

"But you never wanted her before! Besides, it wouldn't be in her best interests. What do you know about taking care of a little girl?"

Troy raised his eyebrows. "What do *you* know, Della? You're a thousand times less maternal than any woman I've ever known, and I'm ready to be a father. I have been since she was born; I just wasn't ready to do it without you. But now I am."

Without you. I'm ready to do it without you. The words echoed about in Adele's brain meaninglessly.

He's taking Judy from me. He's going to be a good father, and I can't be a good mother, and soon two months will turn to three, and three to four, and he'll try for custody ... and goodness knows he'll get it.

He can get anything he wants with that grin.

Why was she even thinking about his crooked, stupid grin? She didn't like his grin. She really didn't. Not at all.

She took a few deep breaths, focused on his mustache—one part of him she really did detest with all her heart. There. She hated him again. She could fight this fight; she could keep Judy away from Troy.

She wouldn't be the victim. She simply would not.

"I've heard that Europe isn't safe." At least, that was what people she assumed were rampant extremists said. That war was coming. She always rolled her eyes at them. There would not, could not, be another war.

The world was sick of wars. Surely it must be. No one in their right mind would voluntarily enter another one.

If there was one thing Adele hated more than being a victim, it was war. War made everyone a victim.

"Europe is safe. At least for now. I wouldn't have taken you for a doomsayer, Della-bell." He winked.

"I'm not. And I told you—I allow Della because you don't have the ability to be a normal person and use my real name, but Della-bell is not all right. Ever." She hadn't even told Millie about her childhood pet name, and the loss it now represented. She hated how Troy accidentally brought it up so often. If she didn't know better, she would say it was intentional taunting. However, since she'd shared nothing with him, ever, about past hurts and the way they affected her future, it couldn't be there.

As always, his eyes flashed with curiosity, but he said nothing. "Sure, Della. Sure. Are you only pessimistic when you might have Judy out from under your control?"

"Shut up, Troy. You're just an idiot." She wanted to use stronger words, but she wasn't quite that far gone. Judy didn't deserve to hear the filthy language her mother wanted to use whenever she thought of her ex-husband.

His eyes darkened in a way she hadn't thought blue eyes could. They were midnight now, daring her to say another word in that line of speaking. "Watch it, Della."

"Or what? You'll hit me? Hurt me? In front of Judy, no less?" Adele leaned against the table, glaring him down. "Is that the kind of man my baby needs to be around? Don't tempt me to try for full custody."

"Don't tempt *me.*"

She guffawed. "You know they won't side with you." She was the mother, and as the judge had said all those years ago, a child needed a maternal influence more than a paternal one. Adele had the right to Judy.

"Oh, won't they?" He did stand then, towering over her, and she stepped back without thinking. "Come now, Della. You're an unmarried woman with an unstable job, you flit from man to man, you drink—God knows how much—and you always seem half-starved. Look at yourself—you've lost thirty pounds,

Della!"

She wanted to yell back at him but paused, confused. Was that a compliment? His tone said otherwise.

"No, I didn't mean that positively." He shook his head, and she caught the moment flash of sadness across his face. He looked older now—more worn before, when before she'd thought his deep-set eyes and serious expression couldn't reach a higher level of solemnity. "You think you're getting your figure back or whatever, but really, you're just taking all the beauty out of your body. It's in your face, your form, your eyes. Killing yourself for an impossible standard, ruining your body because you're hurting inside. You're unhealthy and unstable." He looked her up and down then offered a bit of a smile, almost as if he wanted to appease her. "But I won't take Judy from you. Not unless you make me."

She chuckled dryly. "Make you?" She couldn't make Troy Kee do anything. At least, not anymore.

"By denying me access to her. I'm serious, Della. I need to be with Judy now. I've realized the error of my ways." Another crooked grin.

Her heart did an odd little skip which she stilled with sheer force of will.

"Judy will be with me every summer for a few months, and I'll see her whenever I can. I'll be around on the important days—holidays, birthdays, beginnings of school terms, that sort of thing. If you try to take even an hour of my time with Judy away, I will take her from you so completely that you'll wonder if you ever were a mother. She doesn't deserve you, Della—no child does."

There was a fire in his eyes she'd not known could be there—a cold, icy fire, not one of anger, but one of determination and passion. She was afraid then, and at the same time she needed to have the last word, to think of something that would hurt him.

She turned her back on him and walked over the cupboard. She determinedly opened it and picked up a jar which contained tea leaves. "The way you talk about me, I suppose you haven't heard."

"Whatever do you mean? Don't be mysterious. It doesn't suit you as well as you think, *mon malheur*."

Adele wasn't absolutely sure what he'd just called her, but it was something possessive. She rolled her eyes and set a kettle to boil. "It's rather recent, just happened last month, so I suppose you wouldn't have heard it. Oh, and I've left my ring off today—I can't remember where I put it."

She turned around, pretending to search the kitchen for her lost jewelry—truly, she'd set it on her vanity earlier and forgotten it until this moment—but truly she needed to see his face. See if she'd cut a tender spot. He hadn't wanted the divorce; he claimed to still desire her. It should hurt. She wanted it to hurt.

His face lost its color, but his lips were set firmly, and his expression rather passive. It was his eyes that gave him away, though he didn't allow them to meet hers for more than a second. He cut himself another slice of cake and deposited it on his plate.

"Is that so? Well, then. What is it now? You've gone from Collier to Kee to Collier to ...?" He cocked his head and raised his eyebrows.

"Acton."

"Adele Acton. How musical." He fluttered his eyes at her and chuckled softly to himself.

"But they're not married yet," Judy piped up. She'd been sitting at the kitchen table so quietly that Adele had almost forgot she was there save for blue eyes wide with shock over the first fight she'd witnessed between her parents.

God help her, it wasn't going to be the last. Or so it appeared.

"How helpful you've been today, Judy." Troy reached over and ruffled her hair. "Do you want more cake?"

"Yes!" said Judy.

"She shouldn't," said Adele.

"Oh, but she's going to! Every little girl should be sick with cake on their birthday." He cut a ridiculously large slice and set it on Judy's plate. "Now, what were you saying? Acton, Acton, can't place the name. I suppose I wouldn't know him, though. I don't run in your circle. I've never been the type to give myself so thoroughly to immorality as you seem to prefer."

Adele wanted to launch herself across the kitchen

and attack him, but she restrained herself. "Actually, Hal is a good man."

"Huh. Hal. Stupid name, that."

"Oh, don't be petty. You should talk with a name like Troy! And anyway, it's short for Henry."

"Ah, Henry. I never liked that name either." Troy took a big bite of the cake. "This is delicious, by the way. Did Mother make this?"

"Yes. And stop calling her that." Then Adele almost laughed. Troy had just made her protective of her mother. Gosh, she hated him and the tricks he played with her mind. "She's not your mother."

"You're right, she's not; I called my real mother *Maman*. But she's my mother-in-law, which is rather the same."

"It's not, and she's not your mother-in-law."

"Sure, she is."

"No, she's not. You have to be married to her daughter to be her son-in-law, and *you are not*." Adele carefully emphasized every word. "Hal will be her son-in-law soon."

"Whatever." He rose again. "All right, I'm going to stop eating before I'm twice my size and can't get out the door. Wouldn't that be upsetting for you?"

Adele made a sound she was surprised she had in her; it was somewhere between a growl and a moan.

"But I am taking Judy with me to France in a week or so. Keep that in mind. I can do this, Della. I can take her from you completely—or I can take her a bit of the time. Choose your poison." He winked. "Oh, and don't think your tentative marriage is going to change that."

"It's not tentative! We're getting married in September after Judy goes to school. And—"

"Oh, I forgot something important." Troy dropped back into his seat and leaned his elbows on the table. "Judy, may I ask you an important question?"

Judy smiled softly. "Yes, Daddy."

"Would you like to go to France with me and be my baby girl for a few months? You'd make me the happiest man in the world."

A triumphant smile slid onto Adele's face. There he couldn't win. He could whisk Judy off if he wanted, but with her consent? Oh, no. Judy was a cautious child. Overly cautious in Adele's opinion. In this one instance, Adele would win.

Judy would never willingly run off to an unfamiliar place with an unfamiliar man. Especially not on such short notice. In time, if Troy had given it even a few more days, she might have been persuaded, but not now, when he was so new to her.

But Judy nodded. "Of course, Daddy. I'd love to."

"Good." Troy reached over and shook hands with his daughter.

Adele blinked then blinked again. What was happening? Everything was spiraling out of control. Nothing made sense. Could she count on anyone behaving as they normally behaved anymore?

She let Troy catch her expression somehow, for he

The Lady of the Vineyard smirked and nodded her way.

"You'd better get used to her picking me, Della." Troy stepped toward the door and put on his hat. "She'll choose me over you every time, you know. You haven't raised the child to love you or even respect you. You've raised her to patiently bear you and run to Granny when she needs help—or even kindness. I can tell. That's just who you are. Selfish and unfeeling and careless of others' feelings. Goodbye, Della. May you forever get *exactly* what you deserve from this world."

One last carefree wink, and he was gone.

Oh, gosh. What just happened?

Chapter Three

Mother and Aunt Millie were both sitting in Mother's bedroom late into the night, and Judy couldn't help but want to peek. She sat outside the door, her ear pressed against the crack, and listened to her mother and aunt chat.

"I mean, does he have the right?" Aunt Millie asked. "Can he do this to you?"

"Yes, he can. He will. I've ... I've never seen Troy like that, Millie. His eyes ..." Judy could hear the shudder in her mother's silence. "They went right through me. I knew that I couldn't go another step further without him going absolutely insane. I was afraid of him, and more than that, afraid of this change. Before, he never wanted her, or at least, after I divorced him, he didn't make any move to be with her. But it's clear his mind has changed, and once Troy Kee's mind is made up, little can change him or stop him."

"I know, I know. But ... but Adele, Troy really is only doing what he thinks is best for Judy. You have to have some grace for a man who actually tries, even if you may not like the way he's going about it."

Mother sighed. "I'm sorry, Millie, but I just can't have grace for him. He looked me in the eyes, and I thought he would hurt me if I kept fighting him on this."

"You're always so dramatic about these things." Aunt Millie's tone dragged with half of a sigh. "Violence is in every way contrary to his nature. He would never hurt you, or Judy, and if he is harsh, I'm inclined to believe it is more in self-defense than in any cruelty or even any tendency to use force. He knows his rights, yes, and will insist upon them, but not if that meant causing you or Judy any permanent damage. Troy loves you, you know. He always did."

"Oh, come now." Mother's voice laughed, a mocking quality to it that made Judy wince. "You can't believe he does any more."

"I do believe it," Aunt Millie said. "I believe he never stopped caring about you. I believe he stood down when you made him do so, and I'd guess he's struggled mightily with his own grief and stubbornness

54

to make his way back to Judy, but I believe that in his heart of hearts, he's still your man. If you were to make the tiniest concession, you'd have him at your feet again. He'd love you again. I presume even in the face of your lack of faith, he would see your relationship as unbroken and believe he had no cause to separate from you. Isn't that worth all the ... all the happiness in the world?"

Mother sighed. "But I won't make the tiniest concession, Millie. I won't. I *can't*. I'm with Hal now. Can't any of you accept that I'm with Hal, that I love Hal, that he will be my husband this September?"

There was a long moment of silence. "And Judy? How does Judy fit into your new life with this Harrison fellow?"

"Hal! I literally just said Hal!" Her mother's voice was fast and loud, with an edge of the tone that always appeared when Judy was in trouble. "You're being difficult now. You're just trying to make me give him up when you know very well I have no desire to do so. I won't, Millie. I won't. Your negativity means *nothing* to me."

"You didn't answer my question." For the first time Judy could remember, Aunt Millie's tone was hard. Rock hard. Judy guessed that mother had hurt Aunt Millie more than usual.

Judy shuddered. She couldn't believe her beloved auntie was capable of harshness.

Mother cleared her throat, and the next words

were calmer. "Our current plan is that Judy will go to a boarding school in Suffolk. At least for the time being. We'll see after she's a bit older; there are schools in London she might go to then, especially if she does better after a few years. However, when she's this age—and so anxious; she can be dreadfully hard to manage during the school year, as you remember—we wouldn't want her around." Judy heard her mother rise and pace across the room. "It's the only way, you know. Hal and I need to start a new life together, and neither of us particularly want children."

A silence stretched on for an eternity while Judy digested this information—and apparently Aunt Millie did the same.

"You're such a selfish woman." Aunt Millie's voice was still that firm, cold, angry tone. "Careless, unfeeling. Do you think of anyone but yourself? Do you think of what it will mean to Judy to be ripped away from her mother, her grandmother, the only home she's ever known? Do you think of what it will mean to Judy to lose *you*? When already she felt so frightened being thrust into that grammar school, terrified of being left every day. Do you even care?"

"No, I don't care." Mother's foot stamped against the carpeted floor, a meaningless thud of temper that Judy had long ago learned to ignore. "Why should I care? Judy will be fine. She's weak. She needs to build her strength, and you don't give her the opportunity to do so."

"Oh, shut up, Adele! Just shut up!"

There was a moment of silence, and even Judy was frozen in her spot, mind spinning to try to understand, once again, *why*. Why she was never loved, never cared for, when she wanted it so badly. Why her mother would want to send her far away. Why she had to say mean things about Judy. Were other mothers nicer than this? Judy couldn't even imagine what that would be like.

Then Aunt Millie spoke, softly, like she was telling Mother a fairytale she didn't want to hear—and perhaps for that reason, must hear. "I'm sorry. I shouldn't have said that. I'm your friend, and I love you. There was no need for me to raise my voice. It's just hard to see you abusing Judy like that. Don't you realize ... don't you realize what that would do to her? She loves you, Adele."

"Well, apparently I don't love her enough." Her tone was light—she was laughing at Aunt Millie—but Judy's heart went hard and cold.

Her mother didn't love her? Even a little bit? And she was going to send her to some faraway boarding school where she couldn't even have her Granny or Auntie Millie? *Fine.*

Judy rose to her knees then her feet and crept back into her bedroom where she snuggled down on the pillow next to Marilou. Harsh, hot tears seeped out from beneath closed eyelids, but she wiped them away with her fist and sniffled, determined not to muss her doll with the ugly tears—much less give way to her own weakness.

No, she wasn't going to cry. Only *babies* cried. Her mother had told her that often enough, especially on the days when the teacher had sent her home early for weeping too much. She needed to be brave and strong ... but she also needed someone to love her. Wasn't that important, after all? Love? It was the root of all fairytales and the epitome of all of Granny and Aunt Millie's stories about God. Though sometimes Granny's life didn't reflect that spoken-of love, while Aunt Millie's did, so Judy listened extra hard to Bible stories from Aunt Millie.

Still, where there was love, something Judy found herself attracted to like a moth to flame, there was surely hope.

Into the dark, she whispered a prayer. Judy almost never prayed, but she felt like she needed to talk to someone. Perhaps her Granny's God would be up and about at this hour and willing to lend an ear to a lonely little girl.

It wasn't that Judy didn't want to talk to God sometimes. It was just that Mother thought it was silly to pray to a God who might or might not be there. But Granny always took Judy to church and talked to her about God, and Judy liked it. It all made some sense to her. Meanwhile, Aunt Millie's God appealed to her heart in a secret way she wasn't sure she could express properly yet. She just felt it.

But still, Judy didn't usually pray. She was afraid it would make her beloved mother angry. Tonight? She didn't care, and she set her jaw in stubborn rebellion as she folded her hands and closed her eyes.

"Dear God." Judy cleared her throat and dug her fingernails into the backs of her hands. "I ... I don't really know what to say, but I suppose I'd like someone to love me all the way. Not just when it's easy, but all the time. Granny loves me that way, but I can't live with my granny, and Auntie Millie loves me that way, but her flat is too small for a little girl to sleep in. So I guess I'm asking that, if Mother won't love me even a little bit, You could make my daddy love me? I know You can. Granny says you can about do anything." She opened one eye and flicked it about the room, searching for a sign, before closing it. "Anyway, make him love me, and make him want me, please. That'd be nice. Thanks a lot."

She opened her eyes then quickly closed them again. "Oh, and this is Judith Ann Collier from London. Or am I Judy Kee? I'm not sure. But anyway, that's me who's asking for this."

Judy snuggled into Marilou again and was soon asleep.

Judy skipped merrily at her father's side as they

walked down the London street. He was taking her to Aunt Lola's house for lunch, and Judy couldn't be more thrilled. She barely knew her father's sister, but Aunt Lola seemed nice, and Judy was excited to get to know her.

"Now, don't you worry about being on your best behavior, baby. Your Aunt Lola won't mind one bit how you act—she's just proud to have such a sweet little niece." Daddy flashed a quick grin down at her.

Judy scrunched up her nose. She understood what Daddy meant—that she wouldn't be in trouble no matter what she did, or so he said—but she wasn't willing to believe it. Not yet. "I think I'll behave anyway." That was the way to please people, after all.

He squeezed her hand. "I thought you might. You're such an angel."

Judy didn't know about *that*, but she'd allow her daddy to say so. After all, if someone wanted to think she was perfect, why object? It would be a nice change.

They arrived at the Coles' house, and Judy felt her stomach crawling, a thousand small caterpillars scampering about her inside and telling her that there was something unsafe about the situation. She wasn't sure how she'd feel about spending time with her aunt and uncle. It was a new experience for her. But—she glanced up at her father's strong, confident face—she was sure she could do it.

Daddy opened the door and stepped into the red-brick townhouse. Judy's eyes meandered about the foyer, taking in the wallpaper printed with tiny yellow flowers and a small mirror opposite them. Daddy removed his hat and hung it on a hook beside the door.

A beautiful lady, tall and slim with neatly styled red-blonde hair and blue eyes, appeared. Judy could already see the resemblance between her and this woman—it was in their coloring, yes, but also about their noses and mouths. She looked a lot more like Aunt Lola than she did like her mother.

"There you are, Troy, *mon chéri!*" She nodded to Daddy but knelt in front of Judy without any further attention paid to him. "Hello, sweetling!"

Judy clenched her fists to keep from reaching from her daddy. She was old enough now to be polite, like Granny had taught her. Besides, this woman, her daddy's sister, had never been anything but kind to her. "Hello, Aunt Lola."

Lola Cole beamed. "I'm so glad you could see me today! It's been ages and ages since your mother let me come see you, and I'm so glad your daddy brought you to us for lunch. Your Uncle Dave and I both ... We both love you very much, Judy." Her voice had fragmented, causing the last phrase of her sentence to fall apart, and she pushed herself to her feet and turned away.

"Lola! Are you all right?" Daddy's eyes clouded up like a rainy day, and he put a hand on Aunt Lola's arm. "What is it?"

She brushed a hand over her eyes. "I'll tell you later. I didn't ... I didn't want to tell you when you saw me the other day because I knew you had somewhere to go."

"All right, then." He squeezed her arm. "Let's go into the living room. Judy is excited to get to know you better. I know you haven't seen her since last summer, and so many things change in a girl's life in a year. She's gone to school, you know, though she's out now for a rest."

"Of course!" She forced herself to smile, though Judy could still see the sadness behind her upturned lips. Sometimes sadness lingered in eyes even when the person was determined to grin. Judy had seen a lot of that in her short life. "We're going to get on so well, Judy! I hope you like sandwiches, because that's what I managed on short notice."

Judy always had sandwiches and found them boring, but no one with sad eyes deserved that kind of information. "I like sandwiches."

"Good! We'll have cake afterwards. That I did have on hand." Lola winked. "One should always have a good stock of cake, you know."

Judy beamed. She was going to like Aunt Lola, especially since Mother wasn't nearby to whisk her off at the first chance.

Judy enjoyed lunch with her daddy, Uncle Dave, and Aunt Lola very much. She was so excited that they all listened to her and took the things she said seriously and thought she had some important thoughts and feelings, too, just like anyone.

Her mother always thought Judy was silly and annoying. She shushed her and told her children weren't supposed to talk, which Judy didn't much appreciate, given that she had to tell people things somehow. Judy liked people listening to her. It was so dreadfully nice.

Aunt Lola particularly appealed to Judy. She was full of kind words and affectionate hugs, and she didn't much mind it when a little girl wrapped her arms around her waist and gave her a firm squeeze. Even Aunt Millie could be a bit wilty, and Granny was made of starch. Despite being slim, Aunt Lola somehow had more substance to her.

Aunt Lola took Judy into the kitchen with her while she cleaned the plates and let Judy dry. She didn't seem at all apprehensive that Judy would break something; she just handed her a dry cloth and told her to get started.

It was so strange—Judy loved her mother. She felt sure she did. But for some reason, Aunt Lola struck her as a better sort of mother than hers ever had been, and she didn't even have a little girl of her own. As far as Judy knew, it was just Lola and Dave.

Judy's heart had been burdened since what she'd heard last night. Now she had someone to talk to—someone who was sure to listen and understand her. At least, she hoped so, for the caterpillars had left her stomach, and now all she had to focus on was the heavier weight of her mother's words.

The Lady of the Vineyard

"Aunt Lola, can I ask you something?"

"Of course, Judy." Aunt Lola set down her dishrag and turned to face her, leaning her hip against the counter. "You can ask me anything."

"Well ..." Judy wasn't sure how to phrase the question, exactly, but she'd do her best. "If a mother wants to send her baby girl to a boarding school, but the girl doesn't want to go, does she have to?"

Aunt Lola's lips tightened, and she cocked her head. "Why do you ask?"

"Just because." Judy faked an unaffected shrug. She wouldn't want Aunt Lola knowing Mother had suggested that very thing. After all, she didn't want to get Mother in trouble. Not really.

"It depends, Judy. It ... it just *depends*. Sometimes a good mother might ask her daughter what she thinks about it. But sometimes a mother ... a mother doesn't do what she ought." Lola turned to the sink and stared out the window above it for a second. "Sometimes the father just has to be a man, for once in his aimless life, and interfere, no matter how his pride irks at forcing his way into something he wasn't invited to be a part of."

Judy didn't understand that last bit, but she nodded. "So I ... *A girl* wouldn't have to?"

Aunt Lola sighed and shook her head. "No, Judy. I think I can make sure *a girl* won't have to. Though, *a girl* probably won't have to until the summer's over, so let's not talk about it anymore just now. Thank heavens your mother pulled you out of early and hasn't put you back in. There's plenty of time for that later, and I'm not going to fuss. Yet know that *a girl* will always be safe and loved, as long as there is breath in my body—and in her father's."

Judy blinked. It would seem Aunt Lola knew more than Judy had intended to give away. "Can we ... can we not tell anyone? What you told me?" She didn't want her mother to think she was tattle-telling on her. Because she wasn't. She was just curious. And frightened. So frightened that the heavy weight refused to leave even at Aunt Lola's assurance.

Aunt Lola stepped to Judy's side and gave her a big, firm hug. "No, not yet. It's all right. Don't worry, sweetling. Don't you worry! It's going to be all right." She held Judy back by the shoulders. "I know my brother pretty well, and he's been heartbroken for a long time now. He's also not been the kind of man who should have a little girl until the last year or so, because he used to drink some awful things. But he's stopped that for good, and he adores you." Her face relaxed into a smile. "He's going to make sure everything's all right. Trust him—and give him all the loving you can, okay?"

"Okay," said Judy. "I guess I can try, at least."

"Good." Aunt Lola rose to her feet. "Now, let's finish these dishes before the men wonder if we've run off on them!"

The Lady of the Vineyard

Chapter Four

Adele found some of Troy's requests odd, and the oddest so far was to put Judy to bed. She'd rolled her eyes when he'd asked permission to do so that evening.

"She's six years old, Troy. She's been putting herself to bed for years."

A twitch had appeared around the corner of his mouth, a twitch of anger she was sure, but he maintained a pleasant expression. "Nevertheless, I want to get her tucked in and tell her a story and pray with her. Surely you won't deny me that?"

Adele shrugged. "Sure. Do whatever makes you happy." *And stop judging me for normal things! A lot of children her age don't get tucked in. I never did from the time I was five ...* Her mother had had a nanny for a few years and then dismissed her, a vague memory but a sad one. She didn't even know the woman's name—only that she was 'Nanny' and she had been beloved. Kenny had started spending more time with her then—comforting her, writing her letters when he was away at school, confiding all sorts of things in her. Saying that he, too, felt a disconnect from their parents—he, too, was sorry they didn't love them properly.

At least, that was what he said, and Adele had trusted him, even though her father seemed to love her. She sighed and shook her head. Childhood memories could be corrupted. Adele had been alone as long as she could remember, and a part of that certainly included paternal neglect, even if only because he was never home.

Though Kenny had always said that was a good thing. That they could do with less time and attention from their father. Adele wondered sometimes why he'd become so bitter toward their parents—but she never would be able to ask him now, and anyway, it didn't matter after all these years. It was best not to think about it.

She sat out in the living room with a book and a cup of tea and listened to Troy's deep voice rumbling from the bedroom—sometimes a soft chuckle, sometimes a gentle tone she was familiar with, that touched a place somewhere inside of her. Her heart recognized it in spite of herself.

He was gentle, she remembered. A gentle giant, she supposed was the correct term. Tender and sweet and real, and he could kiss her until she couldn't think of anything else.

No, she wasn't going to think about that. What was wrong with her? It was as if she didn't know her own mind anymore—and yet she did. She loved *Hal*.

Why was she experiencing attraction to Troy? Why was she remembering his good qualities—when she knew very well they had never gotten along? He was so different from her. He wanted different things. He was a ... a *stupid* man, really. A stubborn, traditional man who didn't understand her.

She must remember that, even if his handsome face and sweet ways could deceive her for a moment. Even if the way he loved Judy made her ache, even if she wished someone could treat her like that—like she was the world.

Come to think of that, she was familiar with that treatment, but she'd found it smothering. Thrown it away. Her guilt threatened to overwhelm her heart, and she shook it off, tried to concentrate on the novel in her hands. She must hate him or nothing else would make sense.

Troy came out then and took a seat on the chair opposite the sofa. "Sleeping like a baby! What a darling. Somehow, Della, we were gifted, blessed beyond what we deserve, and I don't know why, but I'll spend the rest of my life thanking God for the miracle that is Judy."

Adele sighed. "She is a remarkably well-behaved child." She set the novel she'd been reading aside. "How ... how have you been?"

He arched his eyebrows. "What? Civil conversation, Della? Are you lowering yourself to my level?"

She rolled her eyes. "Please. I'm trying to be a bit pleasant. We ought to learn to talk. We'll be seeing something of each other, after all, won't we?"

"Yes. I suppose so. She belongs to both of us, I guess." He cocked his head. "How have things been for you?"

"Well. Hal has been busy, but you ought to meet him. After all, you'll ... you'll be seeing him a lot more, too."

Troy's smile was forced. "Hmm, yes. He a nice sort?"

"The best sort." Adele smiled. "Troy, I want to say something, and I'm not sure it'll make sense, but I'm going to try. Okay?"

Curiosity entered his face, combined with a kind of anticipation that edged on fear. "Go on."

"I ... I don't think you're all bad, Troy. Not really. I know we parted on awful terms, and I'm sorry I was so abrupt. I'm not ... I'm not sorry I left you. I had to. It was best for me—best for us, and you hadn't come to realize it, but ... in time you would have. Indeed, you probably have." She paused, giving him time to reply.

He didn't. *Fool man.* She was giving him a chance to salvage his pride, but he wasn't going to take it, apparently. Some people liked the self-torture that allowing themselves to regret past choices brought. Adele wasn't one of those people; Troy was.

"What I mean to say, I suppose, is we divorced quickly and left such a ... a ragged tear. We never had ... closure." *You didn't allow me closure by being so passive. By giving up on me. By not chasing me. Oh, Troy, do you know I might have come back to you if you'd fought, even a bit? If you'd claimed me, I might have been claimed. But you didn't. You let me go. Why, Troy? Why did you let me go?*

He didn't speak for far too long, allowing these spiraling thoughts that did no one any good, especially her. Eventually, he cleared his throat. "What is a divorce but a closure?" Troy grinned. "A divorce is rather final in my opinion. A divorce means we're done. And I think, even if I didn't want to, I've accepted that."

"It was sudden, though. It was quick."

Troy's jaw set. "Della, it wasn't sudden. Don't fool yourself. When you learned Judy was coming, you broke my heart by not wanting her when it was the consummation of the future I'd always dreamed of. A wife and children—a family of my own, something that was mine and couldn't be taken away from me, or so I thought. You broke my heart every day afterward when you refused to plan for your child, refused to be a mother. You remember. You barely let me touch you after that, wouldn't let me hold you, kept punishing me and punishing me for a crime I didn't commit—or if it was a crime, and if I did commit it, you were my partner."

Something in her recoiled. *This isn't fair. That's not what happened. I didn't know what I was going into.* Perhaps neither had he. Yet she couldn't resist snapping back at him. "Don't be vulgar."

"I'm not being vulgar, Della. I'm being honest. You broke my heart steadily for nine solid months, then smashed the bits until they were unrecognizable when you called my baby girl—what was it? A little beast?" His lip curled at the memory, and even Adele shuddered at the thought that she had ever dared to say something like that about Judy. Sometimes her daughter could be a burden, but that didn't mean she wasn't a little person.

He continued on, his words sharp and quick. "I was done then, Della, yet I would have remained faithful until my dying day. I intended to keep loving you, and I didn't expect you'd leave me. So yes, it was shocking, and at first it was a bit hard to cope with. My pride was injured; I didn't think you were angry enough to leave—only to go on punishing me eternally. Punishment I could've taken, but not your absence. And yes, I still don't understand some things. I don't know why you took Judy away from me when I was the

72

one who wanted her. I don't know why you couldn't look me in the eye and say goodbye. I don't know why you married me only to throw me off as soon as you grew bored. I know it has something to do with a lot of things you really ought to see a psychiatrist about, even though I know you hate the very thought. But I can only piece together bits of your past from half-sleep pillow talk I barely remember. The 'why' must perhaps always be hazy to me, and I've accepted that."

Adele winced. She hadn't wanted him to know so much about what she was thinking and feeling. Troy always threatened to undo her with his love, and in his hands, knowledge was power.

"But closure? Della, our whole marriage was a series of ends and deaths. You killed it before it even began. So don't you go on about how you want us to have 'closure.'"

There was a long moment of silence between them. Adele didn't know how to break it. He was right, or at least mostly right. She'd thought even until Judy was born that there was still something to fight for, and had wondered since if, once the fog of whatever had seized her after Judy's birth had dissipated, they might have still had a chance if she'd stayed. But perhaps there had never been anything there at all.

She cleared her throat. "I can answer some of your questions if you want." She perhaps owed him that much, and his anger made it clear he needed resolution, even if he wouldn't admit it.

"I don't want them answered. I can't think about it without becoming frustrated, and I don't feel like being frustrated. Besides, I've had some rather bad news today, and I ... I don't need more."

Adele wanted to challenge this, but his eyes were dark, and that catch in his voice was unusual. She cocked her head. "What would that be, Troy? Can you tell me?"

Troy sighed and ran a hand through his hair, standing it even more on end. "My sister, Lola, has suffered a series of miscarriages, the last a few weeks ago. No reason that doctors can identify; they say it's bad luck and to try again, but I can tell it's just about killing her. She told me about her most recent today. It upset her to tell me, and I never know what to say or do when she's crying, though I try."

"Oh. Well, I'm sorry." Adele, having never wanted a baby, couldn't understand why women got so upset over the things, but she knew Lola would be heartbroken. She was always talking about having a baby. Ever since her marriage, she'd been trying for a child, come to think of it, though Adele hadn't paid much attention to the fact that that wish hadn't been granted.. "She's ... she's had several?"

"That makes seven. One a few months after the trial—the hardest one, actually. She was at four months, could tell the gender." Troy's jaw tightened. "I would have been the proud uncle of a baby boy."

Four months. A vague memory of being told her

baby was the size of an avocado surfaced, a fruit which always made her nauseous and never more so than then. She remembered being irritated at Troy for endless jokes about the baby-fruit comparisons— "Della, if it comes out overripe, can we return it?"

"The next a few years ago," he continued, "and then several within a year. Yet Lola insists that she can carry a child to full term." Troy swallowed. "My sister is a very brave woman, Della. She was complaining to me today that, at a doctor's recommendation, Dave has refused to be her lover for a time, and she's *mad* at him. She thinks it should be in God's hands, not in her and Dave's."

She resisted rolling her eyes, her fingers restlessly drumming against the fabric of the armchair she sat on. "Brave—or stupid."

Troy glared but not too sharply. She could tell he was torn on the subject. "There's nothing 'stupid' about wanting to be a mother, Della, but you're right that she must eventually see the risk. Let's not talk about this. It's too raw. Change the subject."

"All right." Adele glanced around the room. "Um, how are things in Europe?"

Troy moaned aloud, but there was laughter in the sound. "Honestly, aren't you a ray of sunshine? Can't you think of a thing to talk about that isn't morbid?"

Adele leaned forward. "Well, for one thing, I really do want to know if it's safe for Judy in France. I'm serious. I'm not winning any awards as a mother, but I want her to be safe. Please tell me everyone's just being negative." As much as Judy's safety, she feared for her own. She didn't want another war. She couldn't bear it; she *couldn't*.

Troy's eyes flickered about the room, restless, and he leaned back in his chair, rolling his shoulders. "For now, it's safe, but I can't promise it will be forever. However, I keep a close eye on things, and if anything starts to go sour, Judy comes to England and to you as fast as I can manage it. I won't let her be hurt. I can promise you that. I'd die first. There won't be any risk for her because I will not let there be."

Adele gazed into sincere blue eyes for a moment, then shook the rather odd thoughts about the man before her away. *It's too late for me to be thinking about him.* "All right. I trust you. As long as you're cautious. But please do be cautious, Troy. Remember ... you're not the only one with no friends but Judy." She offered a bit of a smile. "I have Hal, but other than that, Judy is most precious to me. Millie runs a close third, of course."

"Of course." Yet his voice held a hint of skepticism. Troy rose. "I'll see you later. I'm ... I'm glad we had this chat. I don't know that I needed closure, but ..." He sighed. "I don't know what I needed. But I've got it now."

Adele rose and crossed the room, extended her hand to him. "We'll have to get along. As you said, Judy is ours—not just mine and not just yours. We'll have to raise her together, albeit separately."

An odd little grin quirked about his lips, and he took her hand and shook it. "Together separately. So strange."

"Divorce is strange." Even Adele could admit that. She had meant to smile at him until he left, parting on a friendly note, but that smile faded as he didn't release her hand, but held it in his palm, turned it over, regarding it. His thumb brushed over the back, made her hair stand on end, made her pulse jump in a way it had no right to do, especially with him.

"It is strange. It's so ... so unnatural. To part when your instinct is to still feel oneness and intimacy." His voice held a gravel tone she didn't know what to think of.

Lust. It's just lust. I know that feeling well, and it is something I can control. It is something both *of us can control.* "It is ... it is rather unnatural, I suppose." Her breath was short now, and she couldn't meet his eyes. She was afraid to meet his eyes. If she did, she would see something in them she didn't want to see, then her gaze would wander down to his lips, and he'd lean close.

She withdrew her hand and stepped back. Even though Troy had been her husband, she was currently engaged. Even Troy wouldn't want to touch her, not really, when she was promised to another. Didn't he still adhere to those strict morals? "Hal will be by tomorrow when you pick up Judy. He's taking me out while you have her. So you'll meet him then."

She was able to meet his eyes then, with the connection broken, and she found them to be somewhat confused, as if he didn't understand why she'd brought another man into the moment. As if he, too, didn't know what to do with his emotions at the present.

That was all right. Emotions could be messy when it came to divorce. She'd been told that often enough. But in the end, her heart would bring forth the truth—that she loved Hal Acton and would be marrying him this September. She could not be wildly attracted to Troy Kee. That she could most definitely *not* ask him to stay the night with her. It would be cheating on Hal to do so, and that would be, well, wrong.

"So I'll see you tomorrow, then."

"Er, yes. Yes, tomorrow." He stared at her for another moment then went to the door. "Lock it when I'm gone." He met her eyes for a moment, and she knew what he meant. *I might come back to you, Della, if you don't. I might ask you to do things I know we'll regret in the morning.*

That was right. They'd both regret it.

"I will," she whispered.

The door was shut and locked, and the temptation removed. She shook her head to clear it, then rolled her eyes. Had she really even considered it? Maybe her devotion to Hal wasn't all she'd thought it was. Yet it must be, for she didn't have room for Troy in her life.

No, she most certainly did not.

The Lady of the Vineyard

Chapter Five

Troy arrived at Adele's flat at ten the next morning. He had wanted to be there an hour earlier, having promised Judy he'd come see her that morning first thing, but he needed a bit more time to chastise himself.

Last night, Adele had glanced at his lips not once but twice in the space of five minutes, a clear cue as far as he was concerned. Further, she'd let him touch her for the first time in over six years without pushing him away. He didn't think she was entirely aware of how she had acted, but she had at least seen how dumbstruck he was by the small intimacies she had allowed. Adele knew how badly he wanted her. Was it in her to tease him, just to see if she still could? Probably.

Troy walked the streets until he was exhausted, his mind a whirl of thoughts. He wasn't going to let her leave him again. If they didn't get together, she couldn't leave, so they wouldn't get together. There would be no fling. Flings did no one any good. Besides, think how crushing it would be to Judy—not to mention the moral implications. He must think of her as no different from any woman. His resolutions there was unshakeable—it should be no different with her. *She's not my wife.* If he repeated that enough, he might just begin to believe it.

Now arrived at her flat with fresh resolve, he knocked on the door, and Judy answered a second later.

"What took you so long, Daddy? I've been waiting and waiting!" She stepped forward and wrapped her arms around his leg.

He bent and gave her a firm hug. "I'm sorry, baby." He'd have to remember how much power small decisions of his had to crush Judy. All the more reason his self-control was so important. *God, give me strength. Hold me close, and don't let me ruin this sweet relationship with my little girl.* "I'm here now. I have a bit of an outing planned for us. Are you ready?"

Judy wrinkled her nose. "*I'm* ready, but Mother says you can't take me until you meet Mr. Hal. All right?"

Ah. Right. He had to meet the fiancé. Was this Adele's way of reminding him that she was claimed? She didn't need to worry. He wouldn't be with her unless she was willing to commit to a marriage lasting to the end of their lives. He didn't need a reminder that she was engaged; he remembered it every second.

Besides, she should know his resolve would only strengthen with testing. At least this meant she was on his side, in a way, though. She wasn't deliberately trying to tempt him; it had been an accident—and perhaps a bit of his imagination rushing in where she wouldn't have anticipated. If he could blame himself, that would be easier, for he could control that. Adele? She was impossible to influence one way or the other. Her heart was far too hard to be touched.

"Daddy?" Judy tugged at his sleeve, bringing him back to the moment. "What is it? You look sad."

Troy shook himself. "I'm fine. Yes, yes, I'll meet this Mr. Hal." He squeezed her shoulder as he rose, and she led him into the kitchen.

There was something satisfying about finding out that his ex-wife's fiancé was a good head shorter than him. He shook Hal Acton's hand, told himself not to make any flippant remarks, and made casual chit-chat about the weather. That was fine. He could handle that.

Out of the corner of his eye, he watched Judy. Hal hadn't acknowledged her since she entered the room, and she was sitting in abject silence at the table, head bowed, hands clasped together in her lap.

The Lady of the Vineyard

His beautiful baby girl was being ignored.

At last, Troy managed to whisk Judy off. He wanted to take her away forever, not just for the afternoon. No child deserved to live with a person who thought children were worthless. Especially Judy.

~

"Do you live in Paris, Daddy?" Judy asked as she sat next to her father on a park bench feeding the birds bread crumbs and enjoying a big box of chocolates. They'd escaped Mother and her man as soon as they could and come straight here, after the brief stop for sweets. She'd been so anxious for him to come, for Mr. Hal wasn't someone she liked in the slightest. There was something about him that was at once frightening and irritating.

"No, baby. I live near the French Riviera. Do you know where that is?"

Judy scrunched up her nose. "It's the place where rich people go on holidays." Granny had friends with houses there.

Daddy laughed. He stretched out one long leg with a breadcrumb resting on the toe of his shoe. "I own a vineyard there, as you've probably heard." His voice was nothing but a breath. "It's a beautiful place."

"Oh," Judy said in the same whispered tone.

"Your mother didn't like it. She said it was a fine place to visit but not to live. Missed her friends and was too busy pouting to make new ones. I think it was too hot for her; she was always fretting." A smile quirked about his lips. "I don't know if it really bothered her or not, as sometimes I think she likes to complain just to see what will happen if she does."

A sparrow hopped forward, snatched up the crust from Daddy's shoe, and flew away. He straightened and turned to her, eyes sparkling.

Judy felt like laughing from the joy of it, but she had questions to ask first and couldn't let herself be distracted by anything, even birds. "Did you miss us after we left?"

"I missed *you* even if I was too sorry for myself to do anything until now. I was a fool, a fact for which I am deeply sorry, but I'm much smarter now." Daddy gave her shoulder an affectionate squeeze. "I love you, Judy, and don't you forget it. I certainly missed you more than this Acton fellow would. Say, where'd she pick the man up?"

"They met a while ago." Judy threw a breadcrumb up in the air and shrieked with delight when a bird caught it before it hit the ground. "Dancing, I think. He's a businessman, though; Mother says he's important. He does a lot of things, and talks to a lot of people, and I'm not allowed to come to his parties."

Daddy made a sound somewhere between a cough and a growl; she patted his arm in sympathy. "And how did it happen that Miss Collier settled on Mr. Acton?"

Judy didn't know what he meant, nor was she

sure if he wanted her to reply, but she did her best, anyway. "I don't know. He ... he didn't leave like the others. Mother always has lots of boyfriends, but for some reason, she kept Hal." Judy shrugged. That was really the best she could do in terms of an explanation. She didn't understand Mother, either.

"Interesting. Lots of boyfriends, you say?" There was a tightness to her father's voice that Judy didn't quite like.

"Yes, lots. She'd stay out all night with some of them." At least, it'd seemed like that for a little girl waiting and waiting for her mother to come home. Perhaps it hadn't truly been all night, but it had been at least until Judy fell asleep. Sometimes Aunt Millie would come sit with her, but her mother didn't always allow it.

Daddy jumped to his feet, causing pigeons and sparrows to scatter, and paced a few steps away before returning to the bench. "Hmm." Then he roused himself and said, "Now, how about some ice cream?"

"I think that's a good idea."

"I'll be leaving tomorrow, if you remember," Troy said when he dropped Judy off at Adele's flat that evening. "I expect you to have Judy packed and ready by the time I get here in the morning."

"Yes, I've got a few things in her suitcase." By her glare, Adele was frustrated with him again for some reason.

Troy didn't want to think about it. He just wanted her to leave him alone and let him take his daughter home to France. He couldn't think about Adele anymore. It was infuriating, and he couldn't stand wondering exactly how close she was to this Hal Acton fellow—and other men.

He knew she could be amoral and unscrupulous, and she didn't see value in anything sacred. Granted, Troy had spent most of his twenties acting like an idiot, but he had recognized that some things were above and beyond his understanding, some rules too sacred to break. Adele held to none of his previously-hypocritical, now heartfelt standards. What was stopping her from doing all sorts of things that made his blood boil?

It shouldn't hurt. It was her right, her decision. Yet it did hurt. It hurt terribly. Someday he'd learn to ignore the tricky feeling, but that day had yet to come. God help him, he was hopelessly jealous. He cringed inside at the thought of another man touching her, even kissing her.

Yet surely he was no longer the only one. He tortured and fooled himself when he tried to believe so. Adele was a modern woman, after all. He couldn't expect to compete with her modern morals, such as they are. That wasn't what he was offering; it never had been.

So why was she tying herself down to Hal Acton? What did he offer her that Adele didn't? Was it just the small differences in the men themselves—or was it more than that? Would she just leave him, too—and her next husband, and her next?

Troy had to get Judy away. Clenching his jaw, he tipped his hat at her. "All right. Thank you." He knelt to hug Judy and left.

After Troy left the room, Adele sat on the bench by the window and watched him make his way out onto the street and down it. As he disappeared, she leaned back from the window and pulled the curtains closed.

She'd been comparing Troy to Hal all day, since she'd seen them together that morning. Their manners and actions and words—their looks, of course. She wasn't without human feelings. Mind and hearts were fine, but a nice face and a better body was nothing to ignore.

Troy kept winning battles in her heart, and it wasn't fair. It wasn't all attraction—it was his laugh and his personality and the way he met her eyes without wavering, unashamed now of himself or of the things he brought to this world. Oh, why couldn't she live with the decisions she'd made? She loved Hal. She did. She was just confused. Hal was a good man. He didn't deserve her unfaithfulness, even in her mind.

Any more than Troy did?

Leaving the living room behind, Adele walked down the hall and lingered outside the door of Judy's bedroom for a moment before heading to bed. There, she forced herself to sleep despite her spinning thoughts.

At seven the next morning, Troy took a cab from his hotel to his ex-wife's flat. Arriving, he knocked on the door, then proceeded to let himself in.

Judy sat on a suitcase in the little foyer, Marilou resting on her lap. She stood and grinned when he entered, almost swaying from the weight of that big, cumbersome doll.

"How soon can we go?" She was bouncing on her toes and her grin was the biggest he'd ever seen.

"As soon as we say a proper goodbye to your mother." Troy needed to separate himself from Adele, yes, but that didn't mean he hated her—and he didn't want to take Judy away from her, either. Judy needed a mother, and if Adele could become that mother, Troy would be more than thrilled. She was, after all, the woman Judy needed. Adele should at least be allowed to say goodbye to Judy.

Judy screwed up her nose and cocked her head. "I already did that. She's in her room now. She said she didn't want to see you again."

He blinked, wondering why, but then it came to him as he stared at Judy. Adele might pretend to be cold and without feeling, but she loved her daughter. She must. There was no other reason for her to have taken Judy from him. So he arrived at a conclusion: "She's probably afraid she'll cry."

"Mother doesn't cry," Judy said.

Troy wasn't surprised that Judy thought so, but he knew his ex-wife a little better than that. "Oh, yes, she does. She cries when she realizes she's made a mistake. If she saw you walking out of this door with me, she'd know that she *has* made a mistake."

"Has she?"

Troy smiled and squeezed Judy's shoulder. "Yes, in not showing her daughter that she loves her." *Or at least I hope she sees the error, the cruelty, the injustice. Judy's too much of a sweetheart to not be smother-loved.*

"Does she?"

Troy sighed and ran a hand through his hair, standing it on end. "I think so, Judy. I hope so! You stay here. I want to talk to your mother, all right?"

"All right," said Judy, sitting down on her suitcase again.

Troy walked to the door of Adele's room and tapped on it. "Della, can I come in?"

"No," came the answer. Her voice was shaky; he'd been right. "I thought you wanted to get an early start; you'll miss your train."

He grinned to himself. "I have thirty minutes. I came early to make sure you had her ready." Sometimes it could be hard to tell with his Adele.

"I have her ready."

"So I saw."

"Why are you still here, then?" She opened the door and glared at him. Her eyes were red-rimmed, and he almost, *almost* pulled her close, almost cradled her head against his shoulder, almost begged her to be his again. *Almost.*

"Because I need to speak with you." He kept his voice gentle. He knew a woman who was breaking when he saw one.

"About what?" Her voice cracked around both words, and he couldn't help himself.

He reached a hand out to her. "Della." He said her name, then stopped for a moment, watching her. His own voice trembling when he spoke. "I wondered ... would you come with us?"

She blinked. "Come with you?"

He smiled. "Yes. With me and Judy. It'd be the three of us."

"No!"

He leaned a hand against the doorframe. "Are you sure, Della? Are you really sure? I'm not God, and I can't always offer second and third and sixteenth chances. I'm not sure if this won't be your last." *Della, you'll kill me if you keep rejecting me. I need to be your first choice. Please don't make me beg.*

"I hope this *is* my last chance." Adele narrowed her eyes. She was resplendent in her anger. "I told you everything was over between us. I told you that if you let me have Judy, you could have everything else; I didn't even ask for financial support. And now you come to take even her from me."

His jaw tightened. She'd twisted that story. "You haven't taken any steps to stop me."

"I didn't dare to! I would be more sure to lose her that way than any other. She would resent me for keeping you away. Like me, she prefers something new while it is that—a novelty. But she'll always return, Troy. You can count on that."

There she was again, changing the narrative to suit her. He ought to ignore her—but he couldn't resist replying. "Will she, if the new proves better than the old? I wouldn't count on her choosing you, Adele. Judy has an eye for quality and will always take it."

"Quality! Oh, for heaven's sake! She's six, Troy, and you're conceited if you think you're better than me. You're not." She started to close the door, but he held it open.

"Della, I wouldn't risk losing so fine a girl as Judy. Yes, she's yours for most of the year, but what about her heart? Don't lose her heart, Della. I know I will never repeat that error. Not when life can be so short.

Come with us." There. He'd given her another chance. She just had to sacrifice her pride. It was the sensible thing to do.

Yet her face didn't soften, and she didn't accept the hand extended to her. "No. I'll never bind myself to you again. It would be suicidal."

His chest tightened, and he forced all his emotional aches away. He'd be sensible about this. "Very well. I'll see you in September." He turned away from the door.

Adele stepped out and followed him to the foyer, but he paid no heed. He simply picked up Judy's suitcase and took her hand.

"We're going," he said. "Say goodbye to your mother, Judy."

"Bye," said Judy airily.

"Will you telegraph when you get to France?" Adele's eyes were big now, and Troy knew it was killing her from the inside out.

But it was too late. "We'll be sure to." He gave her a tight nod, one last look, and ushered his daughter out the door.

After they left, Adele made herself a perfect breakfast—missing Judy's burnt toast and heavily-sugared tea immensely—and went across the street to open the shop, arriving before Millie, who generally opened the shop first thing in the morning before heading to her office job.

She wondered how long it would be before she stopped feeling bereft. Never before had she realized how much Judy played into her life. How she would sit on the counter and chat with the customers, or run next door to Mr. Tilney's grocery, or fly up to her flat to fetch a book which she'd coax Millie to read to her when she should've been working.

Judy was Adele's life. Not her friends, not her fiancé, not her work, not her play, and certainly not herself.

Judy.

Millie arrived at the flower shop and spent thirty seconds staring at Adele before quietly going about her daily business. Adele guessed that she had an idea that something was wrong, but her best friend knew when to keep silent.

Halfway through the morning, Millie finally spoke. "Troy took Judy to France today, didn't he?"

Her throat tightened, but she forced the reply out. "Yes."

"Do you want to talk about it?"

Talk about it? When it was still raw? Yet it might help. Still, she wasn't quite ready to commit to openness, even with her best friend. "I'm not sure."

"All right, tell me if you do."

At last, Adele sat down at the counter and faced

Millie. "I just ... I'm rather used to Judy, you realize."

"Yes. You do rather, er, get *used* to your only daughter." She smiled. "But you'll get her back in September. I know that probably seems like a long way away after you're so very *used* to someone, but it'll be over, and you can make it up to her."

"I don't know what you mean."

"I mean, Adele," Millie said, "you've never been the mother Judy desperately needs. But you can change. You can be her mother, and you can treasure her, and you can show her what it is to be loved. You don't have to lose her to Troy."

She scowled and crossed her arms. "I'm not afraid of that."

"Yes, you are, Adele! I wish it were all because you adored your daughter, but I know part of you is afraid of losing that control over Troy, too." Millie placed an arm on her best friend's shoulder. "Look. I know it was difficult for you when you were small. Don't think I didn't notice how things were for you as a child. I know your father and brothers' deaths broke your heart. I know your mother has ... has acted terribly towards you ever since, for no apparent reason—though I also know you can't understand another person's heart. However, that doesn't give you an excuse to spend the rest of your life bitter and hateful. I know you feel like you must avoid being dependent on others, that you must take control of every circumstance, every person, and even yourself in a cruel way. But it isn't right."

Adele cast her best friend a wry look. "Are you quite finished?"

Millie paused and adjusted her glasses. "Yes … yes, I am. For now."

"Good." Adele offered what she hoped was a sunny smile. "I thought for a moment you were going to run off on another rant about how Troy was perfect for me and I ought to go back to him."

Millie winced. "It's hard not to speak the truth to you, Adele. I love you, after all, and I know Troy can only help you."

Adele smirked. "That's what he thinks. He asked me to come with him and Judy today. Said it was my last chance." She rolled her eyes. "He knows very well I don't want him. I don't understand why he must throw himself at my feet again and again."

Millie stared at Adele in silence for a moment before speaking. "Adele, you're insane. He offered you a second chance at life! Why couldn't you take it?"

"Oh, Millie, leave me alone."

"I will. I'm sorry. But you disappoint me, Adele. You really do." Millie sighed. "I'd best get to work. I'll see you tonight, probably."

Chapter Six

Paris, France

"I like France," Judy said cheerily from behind a large box of chocolates. She sat in the back of a taxi with her father on the way from the train station to their hotel, lightly tapping her heels against the underside of the seat.

Daddy laughed at her but in a happy sort of way that she didn't mind. "I'm glad. I want you to love it here, though I suppose we ought to not have chocolates every day."

Judy disagreed, but it was impossible to get

grown-ups to understand the necessity of chocolate.

The cab stopped in front of a small boarding house that looked tiny next to the huge, grand hotels they had passed on the way. Daddy jumped out then reached back for Judy, the chocolates, and Marilou.

Judy examined the weathered gray building with interest. "Where are we?"

"This is the home and business of my dear friends, Monsieur and Madame Lecroix. It's a boarding house, but they keep an extra room open."

"Why are we here?"

"I always stay with them when I'm in Paris." Daddy fetched his and Judy's suitcases, giving Judy the candy and Marilou to hold—which nearly toppled her over. He paid the driver, and they hurried up the steps and knocked on the front door.

A chubby little girl about Judy's age answered. She beamed up at Daddy when she saw him. "Monsieur Kee! *Tu nous as manqué!*" The girl bobbed a quick curtsey, her eyes dancing.

"*Parlez anglais s'il vous plaît*, Colette. It has been *far* too long." Daddy grinned and turned to Judy. "This is my daughter, Mademoiselle Kee. Judy."

"Ah, *oui!* I have heard so much about you, Judy!" Colette repeated her curtsey.

"I'm glad to meet you, too," said Judy, unsure if she should imitate Colette's quaint gesture or not.

"Come in the house!" Colette led them into a largish foyer with red carpets, an oak desk, and a grand staircase rising from it. "Your room is ready, Monsieur Kee. May your daughter stay in our room, perhaps?"

"If Judy wants to, and your mother doesn't object, I don't see why not."

Judy wasn't sure how she felt about staying with strangers, but if her father thought it was all right, it must be all right.

Turning away from the door, Colette ran to the bottom of the stairway and shouted up. "*Maman!* Monsieur Kee is here!"

Out of a door at the top came a round, middle-aged woman with messy, graying black hair and twinkling dark eyes. She held a baby under one arm, and led a child of three or four by the hand. "Troy, *chéri!* We are honored, once again, by your presence!"

"I'm glad to be here, Madame Lecroix. Is my room available?"

"Naturally! I have the key somewhere." As she scurried down the stairs, Madame Lecroix began rummaging through the numerous pockets of her dress. She found a baby bottle, several coins, three handkerchiefs, and a small notebook, each of which she exclaimed over. She then bustled to the desk and dug through papers until she found the ring of keys.

"There, these are mine to give to the boarders! My husband keeps the master keys—he knows I would lose them!" Madame Lecroix laughed heartily at this. She handed Daddy a small silver key. "Now, don't *you* lose it!" She waggled her finger at him. "Gaston! Louis!"

The Lady of the Vineyard

Two stout little boys ran into the room. They both grinned broadly when they saw Daddy.

"Take the Kees' luggage upstairs. *Vite, vite!*"

The boys hurried to do as bid. Daddy laughingly removed their caps and put chocolates in them as they passed.

"*Merci*, Monsieur Kee!" they cried as they disappeared up the stairs.

"I suppose your husband is still at his breakfast, Madame Lecroix?" Daddy asked as he followed the lady and her children up to the second floor.

"Yes, Troy. He still takes longer to chew than any other man in the world."

Daddy chuckled. "Good! I was afraid you would change, which would of course break my heart, but none of you have."

"The boys are growing."

"So I saw! But I meant on the inside. I don't care how you look."

"You'd change your tune if we remodeled your room, as we have threatened to." Madame Lecroix winked in his general direction.

His mouth dropped open and his eyes widened, though Judy didn't know if it was real or not. "Well, that's different. Atmosphere in a room has a great deal to do with the way it looks. If you were to remodel it, the smell would leave, too, and the feel, perhaps. All my senses would be offended."

"What strange ideas you have, Troy." Madame

Lecroix shook her head in amusement.

"It's true, though." He entered his room where the boys were neatly removing his clothes from the suitcase and placing them in the closet and dresser drawers. Judy was surprised, but she supposed if Daddy came here often enough and was such a good friend, it made sense that the boys might help him out in that way.

The elder of the two removed a small package wrapped in brown paper, undid it, and put the object on the little bedside table. It was a picture frame. Even from a distance, Judy knew who the person in the photograph was.

"Mother?" To the best of her knowledge, all images of her father had been burned. At least she'd never seen one around her mother's flat, and Judy could never get Mother to talk about him. So why would her father have a picture of her mother?

"Yes." Daddy smiled, picked up the picture frame, then set it back on the bedside table an inch to the right. "I think that's all we'll be needing for now. Thank you, boys; I can finish the unpacking."

Gaston and Louis left, closing the door behind them.

Daddy stood by the nightstand, hands in his pockets, looking at the picture. "I don't suppose Mother has a picture of me? No, of course not. Not my Della. She believes in totally eradicating a person from her life."

He'd asked a question and then answered it. Judy

wasn't sure how to respond.

"You see, Judy, I just … I needed something to live for. I was too afraid to love you as I ought, so I loved your mother. Even if I couldn't see her again, and even if she didn't love me back." His fingertips traced the frame, and he seemed to want to say something more, but he simply ended with, "She's a beautiful woman."

"She's the most beautiful in the world." Judy puffed up her chest. There were so few things she could be proud of; at least her mother's looks were one of them.

"Sometimes I'll get irrational and wonder, 'Why is she laughing at me behind the glass? Does she think my pain is some sort of joke?' I know it's silly." He cocked his head. "She laughs at things she oughtn't to sometimes, but she was never … she was never cruel in that way. She could say things that tore deeper than bullets, but she never taunted me. Not exactly."

Judy crossed the room and slid her hand into her father's. "I wouldn't hurt you," she whispered. "I love you."

Daddy glanced at her, a smile quirking up one side of his mouth. "I know, Judy. I love you, too, very much. You're my second chance at life, you know."

Judy nodded. "I'm glad. Do you think you could be my second chance, too?"

Daddy chuckled. "Yes, Judy, I think I could be. I hope I am. I'm not going to give up on you, you know. I'm going to stick with you no matter what."

"Okay," said Judy.

The Lady of the Vineyard

Chapter Seven

London, England

Adele had been playing with her food for an hour now. She sipped at her water and poked her salad around and twirled her fork around her fingers, but she couldn't meet her fiancé's eyes across the table.

"Adele, are you finished?" Hal's look, complete with arched eyebrows and pursed lips, indicated both worry and confusion.

"Um ... yes, I am." She stood, caught up her jacket and draped it over her shoulders. "Let's go home."

He stood, too. "Do you want to dance?" His eyes

were hopeful.

"No. It's late." Or at least it felt late. Her days were so slow now; they crept on and on, meaningless and dull.

He placed a hand on her arm. "It's hardly ten yet, love. Are you ill?"

"No, but I'm tired. I want to get to bed early."

"Very well." Hal had fear in his eyes, but she couldn't reassure him. There were a lot of frightening thoughts flitting through her mind just now. She was afraid, too.

Hal paid the tab, and they began the short walk from the little café where they'd had dinner to Adele's flat.

"Hal," she whispered.

"What, love?" He put his arm around her.

"Do you think we're doing the right thing?"

Hal frowned. "There's nothing wrong with loving and marrying me, Adele. We'd have such a wonderful life together! And we'd have Judy. Judy likes me, remember?"

He knew instantly what she was talking about, which impressed her. She supposed she'd worried often enough about Judy while speaking of the future with Hal. But there were so many things she wanted to give to Judy, so many things that she didn't know Hal could provide.

"She liked you. She won't anymore." She was quite sure of that. "She won't want a substitute father now that she's had the real thing. It's like being offered lemonade after having something sweet. The lemonade was wonderful before, but it just tastes sour after. Oh, Hal, I'm so much in love with you that it'll kill me—I always think it's going to kill me for a while, you know—but ... I mustn't see you again."

His expression hardly changed. "You're being melodramatic." He opened the door to the building and let her walk in before him. "You're confused. You're tired. You're *insane*. Whatever it is, it'll pass."

"I'm not insane, and never before in my life has everything been so clear. I think I know myself for the first time." Not having Judy was clarifying. "I may hate what I am and what I must do if I want to be better, but I'm not acting or thinking unreasonably. You just don't understand."

"The only thing that is clear to me is that I love you, and nothing is stronger than that." His arm slipped around her waist. "You're my angel. I couldn't do without you."

Adele sighed. She began fumbling through her purse for the key to her flat; she found it and unlocked the door. "I'm beginning to think that our kind of love isn't quite as important as people seem to think."

The corners of Hal's mouth drooped like a hound. "Don't say that."

"Why shouldn't I?"

"Because love is all we have that's worthwhile."

"It's worth next to nothing compared to Judy.

She's worth more than something as momentary as 'being in love.'" She paused. Perhaps that was too harsh. She ought to acknowledge that he wasn't a horrible person. "We could've had the worthwhile kind in time, but ... but we're not there yet, and I'm not sure I want to get there with you. I don't know if I like you enough to live with you for the rest of my life, when I know you won't always be young and handsome, when I know you won't always be happy and sweet. 'Being in love' is temporary at best."

"You sound like a parson," Hal complained. "Where's my girl? Are you sure you're all right? You had a glass of wine with dinner. How do you feel?"

"I'm not drunk, if that's what you're getting at." Adele sat down on her couch. "I have been once or twice these last few days, but I'm sober now. The relief is far too temporary, and it gives me a dreadful headache."

"That's because you can't handle alcohol," he said lightly as he paced about the room, touching one thing and then another, before coming to sit down next to her. "You always think you can, but you can't. You might want to limit yourself. Perhaps a glass of wine with dinner every once in awhile ... but other than that, it's probably not the best idea."

"Hal, please." She leaned her head against his shoulder. "I'm afraid, and I need to talk it out."

"All right, love. What is it that's got you worried?" His arm wrapped around her shoulders, and she let herself snuggle into him, reminding herself that she did love him, that he was the man she was going to marry.

Was that even true anymore or did she just keep telling herself that it was? She thought she loved him. Certainly, she felt some attachment to him. She wanted the life he would give her—but only if that life could include her daughter.

"What about Judy?"

"What about her?"

"Are you ... oh, gosh, Hal, are you ready to be a father?" Adele cupped his face with her hand and made him look at her. "Darling, this isn't just an idle game. It's serious. I need the man in my life to be there for Judy as well as me."

"I'll be there for her. I promise."

"Being a dad is so much more than that. You saw Troy, didn't you? You know how he treats Judy, how he loves her?"

His lips twisted. "I know."

"Can you be that man?"

Hal stood and paced about the room, his brow furrowed and his eyes dark. "Can I be your ex-husband, you mean? Because if that is your question, then the answer is no."

"That's not what I meant."

"Yes, but it's what you feel is needed, isn't it?" Hal sighed. "Adele, please, please don't ruin our relationship because of this! It's not that important, really. You're just shaken because you weren't expecting him to come back. You weren't expecting Judy to like him. But it's a passing thing. Look at me." He came and knelt before her, took her hands in his. "I love you, all right?"

His eyes were sincere, and she dropped her forehead against his. "I believe you. I'm just afraid for Judy."

"She'll be fine! Children are resilient." He winked. "Anyway, won't it be better for her to have a father who will be around all the time? A real family?"

"Yes, I suppose so." Yet her heart doubted. Much as she liked Hal, was she making the right decision for Judy ... as well as herself?

Chapter Eight

French Riviera

With many promises to visit again soon, promises she dearly hoped to keep, Judy bid goodbye to the Lecroix family and got on a train with her father that would take them to the French Riviera and their vineyard.

The train ride was thrilling for Judy. There were so many sights to see, in and outside the cars, that she never had a dull moment. Even when the scenery became less exciting, her father's talk kept her busy. Eating in the dining car was another thrill. Her father taught her the French names for everything on the table and got the waiters involved in teaching her the language.

She'd never traveled with her mother, despite the fact that she would occasionally go down to Kent for the weekend to visit Millie's family or some of her own friends. Mother thought taking Judy places was rather a bother, and Judy was always left with her grandmother on such occasions. Though Judy tried her best to understand, it was hard. She loved seeing new places.

Soon the train was flying along the beach. Judy's nose rarely left the windowpane, and she never grew tired of blue sky and ocean, white sand and seafoam. It was beautiful, perfect, and a bit blinding. Judy loved it.

Toward the late afternoon, the train stopped. Judy stepped out. The scent of the sea enveloped her. They walked to the end of the platform, and Daddy pointed out a few of his favorite stores down the street. The town was beautiful. When she said so, her father just laughed.

"Towns are all very well, but it's the country that'll really catch your eye. I can't wait to show some of the sights to you, baby."

Judy grinned. She had never had such a time in her life. But that wasn't really the best part, either. She would have done just about anything with him and been just as happy. She wasn't quite sure why, but it was grand.

Holding Daddy's hand with her left and Marilou with her right, Judy skipped across the platform. A small silver sport car was parked opposite. There a man stood, his arms folded, disapproval showing on every line of his middle-aged face.

"The train was late," were the first words out of his mouth. He had no accent, so Judy guessed that he must be an Englishman. Though goodness knows what an Englishman would be doing in France.

Then Judy remembered she was English and in France and giggled.

Daddy grinned. "I'm sorry, Harrington. I couldn't very well speed it up. I don't control the trains."

"I've been sitting here for half an hour now." His scowl was as deep as the ocean. "I forgot to bring a book. Which is a shame, because I'm right in the middle of *War and Peace*, and I'm never going to finish it at this rate."

"Do you like it so far? Never was able to wrap my head around a book that thick."

"I don't like it. It's dull."

"We agree on something, anyway. Anything that large must be dreadfully boring." He shrugged. "You remember my daughter, don't you?"

Harrington glanced at Judy very briefly before returning his eyes to Daddy's face. "Has she grown some?"

"Yes."

"Oh. Perhaps that's why she looks different."

Daddy chuckled. "You didn't expect her to be a baby still, did you?"

"No. Perhaps I expected her to look less like a little girl and more like an infant."

"Well, she's six now, and I expect you to be kind to her. She's an important person to me." He reached down and squeezed Judy's shoulder.

Harrington merely grunted and turned away. As he gathered up some of the luggage, Troy knelt beside Judy.

"That's Harrington, a good friend of mine. He was my uncle's dear friend before he died, the caretaker of the vineyard afterwards, and now he's a mentor of sorts. Do you know what that means?"

Judy thought for a moment. She wasn't quite sure, but perhaps she knew. "It is a ... a teacher?"

Daddy beamed. "Yes." He took Marilou. Judy was grateful; her bulk was becoming somewhat hard to manage. "Just be careful around him until he falls in love with you, which he will. I've known him since I was a kid myself, and it just takes him some time to warm up to you. He took care of me and your aunt Lola after our parents died during the Great War. He's been a second father to me." He shrugged.

"Will he like me?" Judy whispered.

"He'll be in love with you within a week. But he'll never let you know it. Never. That's not his way." Daddy shook his head in amusement.

"Why not?" Judy asked. "When you love someone,

114

don't you just want to ... to love them hard?" That was how she felt about her mother. She'd give her a world of hugs and never let go, if only Mother would let her, just a little!

"Mm, some people don't always show love on the outside. Like ... like your grandmother. Sometimes, that is. She seems to be open with you."

"Granny and I understand each other." She was repeating a statement of Granny's, though she didn't quite understand what it meant. The feeling seemed to express her general thoughts toward the relationship.

"I think that's wonderful." His eyes were thoughtful. "So you wouldn't want to go long without seeing her, I suppose."

Judy nodded, though she didn't quite understand. After all, she'd see Granny almost every day once she got back to London. She never doubted for a moment that she'd go back to London, though she hated the thought of it more every day, despite Granny.

Besides, if her mother sent her to that dreadful boarding school, she'd never get to see Granny again. Judy felt tears well at the thought.

However, she shook herself and soldiered on, not wanting to sadden this bright day with her thoughts of returning to London, her mother, and then possibly boarding school. Still, it was hard to shake the dreadful thoughts away.

Daddy picked her up and carried her to the car, placing her in the front seat then jumping up beside her. That way, she sat between Harrington and her father. He gave her Marilou, and she cuddled the doll close.

"I'm listening to the engine on the way up," Daddy said. "It'd better not sound worn to me, Harrington!"

Harrington rolled his eyes. "Your firstborn is fine, Troy. I hardly drove it."

Judy wrinkled her nose. Wasn't she her father's firstborn?

"Hardly, but some?" He patted the dashboard. "Who knows what you've done to her? And she's such a tricky thing."

Judy almost laughed. They were talking about the car. "Daddy, it's a car! That's an *it,* not a *she.*"

Daddy grinned and put an arm around Judy's shoulders. "This is a very special car, though, and I'd hate for her—or it—to be ruined by careless driving."

"It won't be." Harrington scowled. "You're too careful of this spitting beast of a machine! It's almost seven years old now—when are you going to trade it in? Don't say you can't afford it, because you can."

"This car, my friend, has tremendous sentimental value," Daddy said, glaring at Harrington, though Judy could tell he wasn't terribly serious. He turned to Judy. "Do you know where I got this car, Judy? Or rather, how?"

Judy shook her head.

"Well, when I arrived in France with your mother, shortly after our marriage, she insisted we buy a car. *All right,* thinks I, *a nice conservative little car that can get us around is probably a good idea.* I'd always walked to the village before, but it's a bit of a hike, so I can see why Adele wouldn't want to." He shook his head. "But of course your mother is never conservative, now, is she?"

"What's that?"

"Er, careful. Old-fashioned."

Judy sighed. "No, she isn't."

"So we bought this car!" He patted the seat beside him. "It cost me a year's pay, Judy, and dipped into my savings worse than anything else. It made her happy, and I was glad of that." His eyes darkened. "Still, you can't just go buying things for people to make them love you. It does no one any good."

"I guess." Judy had been glad when she'd gotten Marilou from her grandmother, but that wasn't the reason she loved Granny. There were many other reasons. So, she supposed, her father was right. One had to love others in different ways than through things.

Especially if the things were shiny expensive silver sport cars.

Though it was quite odd, Judy fell in love with her father's house at first sight.

The Lady of the Vineyard

The steps at the front led up to a veranda. Big windows that nearly reached the floor looked out onto it. Sticking out past the veranda to the left side, another room had been added on haphazardly, and on the other side of the house a balcony dangled from the upstairs.

"It used to make sense, but I built onto it." Daddy's chest puffed out as he spoke. "Do you think you'd like living here?"

"Oh, yes! But I couldn't, of course," she added as she hopped out of the car and grasped his hand.

"Why not?" Daddy asked, smiling softly.

Judy laughed, thinking he must be joking, and tugged him along after her on up the steps. A big yellow dog ran out when the door was opened, barking excitedly and wagging his tail. Judy stepped back, alarmed at his size.

"Hello, Holt, I missed you, boy!" Daddy said, bending over to hug the wiggling creature who, from Judy's perspective, was all tongue.

"Holt?" Judy eased her body behind her father's so proper distance was obtained between her and the big beast.

"Yes. He's big and ugly, but you don't have to worry about him. He'll love you, too." Daddy caught him by the collar to keep him from knocking his daughter over. "Whoa, boy! Sit! Off!"

Holt did nothing of the sort. He wasn't the obeying kind of dog, Judy supposed, just like her mother wasn't the loving kind of person. Yanking away from Daddy, Holt barrelled Judy over, then ran past her to greet Harrington—who kicked at him—and then back to Daddy, who shoved him into the nearest closet.

"He can come out after he's settled down some." Daddy helped Judy up and dusted her off. Thankfully, she wasn't bruised, or if she was it didn't hurt a lot, and she soon felt right as rain.

After exploring the house up and down, Daddy and Judy finally made their way down to the kitchen for a snack.

"What do you think of the place?" he said between biscuits, something which he had thankfully stocked up on. Judy loved biscuits very much indeed, but her mother never had them around. Apparently, they were fattening—and hard to resist. Mother said this was not a good combination.

"It's nice." Judy cocked her head. "The room I'll stay in is pretty, and I like it a lot, but it's a bit babyish." She winced, hoping he wouldn't be too offended, but he simply nodded, eyes thoughtful.

"That's because it was made for a baby." He stood and fussed about the kitchen before returning to his seat.

"Me?"

"Yes. You weren't really expected—at least not for a while longer anyway—so I had to build on that little bedroom off my office. It's an odd corner to shove a baby in, but I was in too much of a hurry to think straight."

Judy blinked. "Oh. I lived here?" She'd always thought her mother had run off long before Judy had a chance to do any living at the vineyard. Though it had been a long time ago, so she couldn't remember or anything.

"No. Not really. I don't believe you ever slept in your room, though you slept in the house. The month you spent here you were in my bedroom, upstairs."

"Because I was so little?"

"Yes, because you were so little."

Judy smiled. "Did I sleep with you in your bedroom?" She was never allowed to sleep in her mother's room, even when the nightmares were particularly bad, and it was always rather scary.

"No. You slept with your mother. *I* slept in your room."

"Why?"

She saw him swallow, saw him hesitate over what to say next. She wondered why. "We quarreled."

"About what?"

He sighed and ran a hand through his hair making it stand on end in five or six places at least. "Oh, a lot of things. It doesn't matter. All that matters now is that we *did* quarrel."

Judy frowned. "I wish you hadn't. Then you could come and live in London with us." Then she wouldn't be alone. With him there, perhaps her mother wouldn't send her to boarding school, and then she could stay near all the people she loved and be loved by them. It would be a dream come true, in short.

Troy shook his head. "No. I don't like London. Big cities don't suit me. You can barely hear God. I grew up in a big city, and I never knew what I was missing until I moved here." He gestured around him. "Here, there is peace and quiet and beauty and truth. I couldn't live in London again."

Judy wrinkled her nose in thought. "Then ... then we could come live here." That seemed the easiest solution. Though getting her mother to agree might pose a rather large and insurmountable issue.

He shook his head. "Your mother doesn't like it here."

"But it's beautiful!"

"'But it's boring!'" he said, imitating Adele's voice.

His mime of a squeaky falsetto made Judy laugh. "I think I could find lots to do here."

"But your mother couldn't. It's all a matter of taste, I suppose." He gulped down the last of his milk. "You almost finished?"

Judy nodded, wiped the white mustache off her upper lip with her sleeve, and hopped down from the tall stool he'd placed against the counter.

"All right. I'll give you a tour of the outside now." He stood, lifted Judy onto his shoulders, and called for Holt—who had been let out after his barking turned to whining. He ducked through the door, narrowly missing banging Judy's head on the frame, causing her to shriek and hold on tight.

The Lady of the Vineyard

Chapter Nine

The ache in Adele's chest at last grew so great that she was forced to set her novel down and sit, hands pressed to her forehead, at the kitchen table, trembling. Usually at this point in the evening, if she didn't have something to go to, she'd end up talking to Judy.

In the last few weeks, she'd been going over to see Millie one very free evening, but her friend was visiting family in Kent. She couldn't have Hal over without expectations. Judy had been her safeguard when it came to the flat; without her here, it didn't seem right to have Judy over.

Her rules for Hal were different than they were for

other men. She wanted to marry him—and that meant she didn't want him corrupted. Not even by herself. Though he'd made it clear his experience was greater than even hers ...

She shuddered. That had never bothered her before. Why was it now?

The truth was, though Adele flirted and played with all types of men, she wanted one who was above average. Chivalrous was the right word—or perhaps moral. Perhaps she appreciated the contrast to herself—she believed herself to be careworn. More and more, she felt old and tired, used up. If nothing else, clean leaving gave one energy. She believed that, even if it wasn't for her.

Around this time of an average night, Judy would stand up and drag her doll to the bathroom. Water would run, and Adele would go to make sure she didn't overflow the bathtub. If she was bored enough, she'd sit with Judy. Her daughter was nothing if not pleasant background noise.

Or that was how she'd viewed Judy for years. It seemed she meant a great deal more than Adele had supposed.

At last she couldn't bear the silence. She rose from her seat and went to the telephone. She hesitated for another moment then took the plunge.

The somewhat tired voice of her mother answered almost immediately. "Hello?"

"Mother, it's me."

"Adele?"

She found herself smiling, perhaps at the pleasure of another person's voice and perhaps out of amusement. "How many children do you have, living? Of course it's me."

"Oh."

A long moment of silence.

"Is everything all right?" Her voice held only the barest trace of concern, but at least Adele thought she detected the edge of it.

"Yes. Yes, it is. I just thought ..." What excuse could she give for calling? She couldn't think of anything other than Judy and Hal—and she didn't want to think about either of those people. Had her mother ever experienced so many scrambled thoughts? "When you were dating Father—"

Mother cleared her throat. "I never 'dated' your father, Adele. I'm not even sure what that means."

"Fine. What would you call the time you spent together before you got engaged?" Actually, Adele didn't know much about her parents' relationship at all. She knew they'd married when her mother was eighteen, her father was several years older, and that her mother had grown up in Kent, but everything else was foggy. "Actually, why did you marry him at all?"

"What a ridiculous question."

Perhaps she'd better attempt this from a less personal angle. "How did you meet?"

"We were often in the same circles in Kent."

Adele rolled her eyes toward the ceiling. "Why can't you just tell me this little thing?"

A moment of silence. "One of my dearest friends—who moved to London long before you were born, when she married—was the sister of your father's current superior, who as you might remember as your Uncle Caleb. I was invited to a dinner party at their home—and there, we met. Your father asked me to correspond with him when he returned to Africa—so I did. I was seventeen then. He came back six months later, and as both our families approved, we were married."

"Did you ... did you love him?"

"I learned to care for him."

"Oh." Her mother never failed to disappoint any hopes Adele had that she might be a woman with normal emotions. "I knew you respected him, at least." Even feared him, though she wasn't sure if she'd imagined that or not.

"I did."

"As did I." That is, she thought so. She'd been so young she barely remembered anything about him. "Why did you decide to marry him originally? If you were close to a family like the Knights, you certainly had other ... suitors? Is that what you had back then?"

The line went silent for so long that Adele wasn't sure their call hadn't been dropped. "Suitors, yes. However, I was young, and he was the only man amongst them. At least, I thought so at the time. I might've made a different decision had I been older—

126

that I freely admit. But he was a strong man, a decisive man, and he gave me two sons who I loved deeply. We remained faithful to each other—we focused on building our family name together. That was what mattered. The fact that it didn't go well was beyond my control."

Adele sighed. Her mother had made it more than clear that she was proud of the life she'd led—that there were no regrets beyond losing her husband and sons to the war. Her relationship with Adele certainly didn't cause her any moments of self-reflection, except perhaps to stir up bitterness and anger.

Yet what could she do about it?

She ended the conversation with her mother as soon as she could after that and returned to the noxious embrace of the quiet. There, her longing for Judy increased.

She didn't want to end up so entirely separate from her daughter's reality that every word she spoke sounded like a foreign language. Yet that was the path she was on.

What would it look like to live entirely for Judy? Whatever that was, Adele was becoming more and more interested in pursuing it.

Even if it meant entirely abandoning all association with Hal Acton.

The Lady of the Vineyard

Judy clutched her father's hand as they strolled along the pavement of the little town near his vineyard. Her eyes widened as she took in the brightly-painted buildings accented by the glowing summer sun. He stopped at a bakery and bought treats, and they sat at a table for two on the sidewalk to enjoy them.

"There are too many people here this time of year," Daddy commented, "but in the off-season, it's quite nice. I know a few people I adore. The Bernards and Laurents. I'll introduce you to them someday. But I mostly observe from a far. I'm sorry about that, truly—I feel like I've alienated myself from true friends. However, I like to limit the special people in my life— just a few families in every city I visit regularly. My sister in London—the Lecroix family in Paris—and of course the Bernards and Laurents here."

Judy nodded and licked thick, gooey chocolate off her fingers. "I can understand that. I don't much like having friends."

He smiled. "Is that so? Why is that?"

"Because ..." She wasn't sure how to explain it, but they were different from her. She hadn't wanted to talk to anyone while she was at school, and then she'd gotten embarrassed and cried. A lot of the time, teachers had sent her own—and no children had approached her. They probably thought she was strange. But even before then, whenever her grandmother arranged for her to play with another

128

little boy or girl, she felt odd about it. Her mouth would seal shut, and eventually, she'd find herself more watching whatever game they were playing than participating. "I don't know. They're Granny's friends' children." She didn't fit in amongst them, and she never would.

Daddy chewed thoughtfully, his blue eyes never leaving hers. "It's all right not to like everyone, as long as you're kind. But I want you to grow into having friendships. You're such a serious, quiet child—and I find that delightful, frankly speaking, but I'm not sure it's good for you."

Judy felt being alone was quite good for her, but she didn't say so. She just finished her pastry.

"We'll keep going to church." Daddy drummed his fingers on the table, his eyes distant now. "Of course, there's Harrington. But I'd like for you to meet more people here. A lot of the people nearby are elderly—their children are long grown. There is a school up the road ... Catholic, though. Hmm. I'll look into it."

For what? Judy wouldn't be staying here when it was time for school. She had to either go to the same awful school in London—or be sent away to the even more awful boarding school which she thought was to the north. Far, far away from everyone she loved. The idea terrified her, but nothing had indicated that she had any say in the matter.

"I'm no model, though. I used to be, when I was younger—or, at least, I interacted with people outside my immediate circle more. I wanted to be more like that—which is why I've maintained my friendship with the three families I am close with." He shook his head, as if jarring himself back to the table he was sitting at with Judy. "If I'm going to be a good father, I'm going to have to keep on being a better person. Which I need God's help with."

Judy nodded. "I guess so."

"Come on." He rose and gestured down the street. "Let's continue on to the beach, baby. I want to show it to you—and we'll go swimming there some other day."

Shuddering in fear at the thought of a swimming adventure, Judy nonetheless took her father's hand, and they continued marching through the tiny, idyllic French town.

Chapter Ten

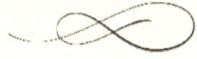

London, England

Hal took Adele to a park for a walk one moonlit evening. She knew it was supposed to be romantic, but she didn't feel like romance just then, and the supposedly comfortable silence that had fallen between them was growing uneasy.

He must know she still had doubts about their relationship. About how he would affect Judy. About what her daughter needed for her happiness, safety, and ability to grow.

Adele wasn't perfect, but she wanted to be a better

mother now—and a less selfish woman in general. She didn't believe she loved herself, exactly, but she did enjoy serving herself. She made her choices based on what she wanted, what she liked, and what she was interested in or excited by.

However, there had been one day about six years ago when she slid her arms under a small bundle and lifted her and looked into a screaming little red face, and her heart had done some priority reorganization.

Yes, she kept a lot of her priorities. Adele, always Adele above all else. After all, no one else would prioritize her happiness. It just so happened that Judy affected a part of her she hadn't known existed, that she tried to pretend didn't exist. She pretended so effectively that no one but her could know of the secret love, and of course, the prioritization.

Now she needed to share that priority with someone. She recognized that need in herself and in Judy ... and if Hal couldn't recognize that need, which he didn't seem to be, perhaps he'd have to stop being a part of her life. Even if she loved him, she knew it was a shallow attachment.

Still, it was a form of love, and she'd always pursued love before, until it ran out, as it always did. Surely she couldn't leave the man she loved and wanted—in the moment, at least—to spend the rest of her life with for her daughter's sake? No. She couldn't. She wouldn't. She didn't believe in that sort of self-sacrifice.

Love didn't have to be like that. Just because she loved Judy didn't mean she should give up someone that meant as much to her as Hal Acton did. He was a man whom she could count on—for a good time, for a happy marriage, for her own ability to rise beyond her demons.

Hal would never force her to show her hidden weaknesses. Hal would not expect her to have more babies. But it seemed that Hal would also never appreciate Judy, and she wasn't at all sure how she felt about that.

Troy—Troy adored Judy. More and more, Adele was thinking about her ex-husband in flattering terms. It made absolutely no sense.

She'd weaned herself of the need for that man years ago, that dangerous need for something clean and wholesome and beautiful. Something that lasted. Something that tempted her to bare her soul to the light of truth and honesty, to the light of true love. What would happen then?

She would fall apart.

No, Hal would never make her fall apart. He was a safe choice, and he'd make her happy. He enjoyed a party as much as she did, too, which was something one couldn't say of Troy Kee.

Cruelly, she told herself that Troy was boring, old-fashioned, annoying, patronizing, controlling, and misogynistic.

Even her thoughts felt like lies now. Couldn't she

hate the man without bending and distorting the truth until it was unrecognizable?

She remembered when she'd faced the truth, that awful year. Without knowing it, Troy had dug deeper into her soul than anyone before. They hadn't had a lot of conversations about her past—she hadn't let him bring it up—but what conversations they'd managed had led to surprising honesty.

She wasn't sure she was ready for honesty. Ready for the fact that, if she had stuck with that man a minute longer, she would have been admitting her problems to him. That was why she'd left him in the first place, wasn't it? Because of her problems?

He'd have to know if she ever came back to him. He'd have to know the quiet places in her soul. He probably would know if they were to spend any amount of time together. She liked talking to him, after all.

He was the first man she'd ever really liked just talking to. Even Hal wasn't that interesting when it came to casual chatting about this and that. They talked romance and dreamy future plans and how much fun they'd had at the last party and the weather, but that was it.

Troy had gotten her talking about religion on their second date. Religion! And that was her worst subject, too.

Yet she'd loved it. Loved how he got her talking, and how he talked to her. It was cathartic. It made her feel better every time, no matter what they talked about. Even casual conversations had been healing, because she knew he loved her, and she knew there was no fear with him.

She could say anything, anything in the world, and he'd still love her.

Oh, she'd said some terrible things to him. Called him the worst names, cursed him, and insulted his life. They'd had horrid quarrels.

Troy had fought back, but never the way she did. He couldn't use words as weapons the same way she did—or at least he didn't. An occasional cutting sentence or two was all she got out of him. He restrained himself, and that made her hate him all the more in the moment—and now, it made her remember him with a grudging respect.

It had driven her mad in those terrible days when they were doing nothing but fighting. She had ended up sobbing herself to sleep some nights, because the scars cut deeper in the person who said the hateful words than the person who heard them sometimes. At least, in her experience.

If so, my mother is cut deep. Mrs. Collier had softened a great deal since Judy came, every day seeming gentler and more caring, but that wasn't the Mrs. Collier Adele knew. The Mrs. Collier Adele knew called her daughter a little demon. A witch. An unfaithful daughter and sister. A slut, as she grew older, and immoral, and wicked.

Words, phrases, sentences Adele didn't want to

remember.

But was it her mother's fault, then? No. It wasn't. She had to stop blaming her mother and the war and humanity for her problems. They were called 'her problems' for a reason.

"Yet for every action, there is an equal and opposite reaction," she whispered.

"What's that, dear?" Hal asked. He put his hand over hers on his arm and smiled down at her.

"Oh, nothing." She didn't think he'd care much about her scrambled thoughts. He didn't seem the type. He might smile and pat her hand and tell her that was all fine, but he'd never understand.

Yet he's from the same generation of me. He knows some of it. He was a small child during that dreadful war, as I was. He may remember losing people.

"Hal, was your father in the war?"

Hal glanced at Adele. "What war?"

"The Great War, of course."

He cocked his head. "Yes, he was in France, I believe. But only for a year or so, and then it was over."

Adele almost laughed at that. She was raised in an army family, and she knew very well that the war never ended in a soldier's mind. It went on forever and ever.

She shuddered. "Was he wounded?"

"No, he survived unscathed." Hal smiled. "You know the old man. If he had a war story to tell, he'd tell it."

Adele barely knew the elder Mr. Acton, had met him all of twice and both only in passing, but she was willing to bet he was anything but unscathed. A man didn't come home from war unscathed, even if his body ended up escaping bullets. There were worse things than bullets.

Yes, war made everyone a victim.

"Do you remember much about the war?" Adele asked. "I remember it all quite vividly, you know."

"You were, what, five?" Hal chuckled. "It can't be that vivid. I don't remember much. All the excitement. My mother being worried. Men coming home heroes. I was jealous of our next door neighbor for his many medals." He tapped his chest. "He was my idol."

Oh. So he only remembered the gilding to the pain and death and horror. The waving banners, the propaganda, the false bravery.

That made sense. If her family hadn't been hit so hard, she would remember nothing but that, too. She would remember the supposed beauty. The grandeur. The fun of being a girl in a world full of patriots, of being swept up in a cause one knew nothing of. She wanted better for her country than that. Was that really so much to ask? Yet here was God again, probably calling more horrors down on Europe. Not that she believed in God. Probably. What proof was there, after all?

"Hal, I know I said I'd like to send Judy to a boarding school after we're married, but now I'm not sure of that." She took a deep breath. "I think Judy ought to stay in London and go to a school here. Somewhere where she can come home to and be with her family every day. It's only fair."

Hal stopped in the path, turned to her, and gave her a very odd look. "Why would you want that, Adele? You know she'll just get in our way." He smiled and leaned into her.

She didn't know why she brushed off his kiss, turned her head, pushed him back. Only that she did, and that right now, the idea of him touching her wasn't a pleasant thought at all. "No, let's talk."

"Oh, all right. I suppose we ought to discuss this." He turned and glanced around, then gestured toward a bench down the path a bit. "Let's sit there."

She waited until he seated himself before lowering herself down next to him. She never let men stand over her when she could help it. She was already so short, and it intimidated her.

Adele hated feeling intimidated. There was nothing more difficult to stand.

She liked to be in charge. She wanted to be the one who inflicted pain, not the one who stood there taking it. She wanted to be the one who left, not the one who was left. She wanted to be the one making the decisions, not the one taking the orders.

A leader, not a follower, but neither did she want people depending on her. She wasn't really sure what she wanted, honestly. Everything had gotten so confused and messy and lost in the shuffle of her own mind.

Now she was afraid that Hal might turn out to be the type to take something away from her, that something being Judy. Just now, she didn't feel like sending Judy away. She'd rather let Judy stay and risk the heartbreak if, some day, Judy hurt her. It seemed a better idea than being the one who hurt that little girl.

"Adele, I love you very much," Hal said, "but I thought Judy wasn't going to be a part of our life. I mean—" He sighed. "Of course she'll have to be a small part of our life. We'll have her for holidays and whatnot. But I assumed we weren't going to have her all the time. Won't she rather interfere with our life? I thought we felt the same about children."

"What if a child comes? Unexpectedly, I mean." He'd have to be a father then, wouldn't he? He wasn't the type to abandon her. At least, she didn't think so. Would she have to leave him, too, to assure she wasn't the victim? No. She didn't want to leave another man. Divorce was too messy.

His eyes softened. "Is that what's scaring you, love? You're not naïve and twenty-two, Adele." He took her hand. "You know now that we can prevent that."

"Not definitely." She shrugged. "I know women who have taken every precaution and still conceived. I could."

"Then we'll get rid of it. For heaven's sake, Adele, you've become a little worrywort." He squeezed her hand. "Shush, now. Why don't I take you back to my flat? It's closer than yours, and you can't say Judy will miss you in the morning now." He kissed her cheek. "Come on. Time to be a grownup about this." He winked.

She sighed. She didn't want to be a grownup. She wanted to be innocent, to not have to worry about such things because she could trust someone no matter what changing scenario took place. Was that so much to ask, really? It must be.

Besides, Adele *wasn't* innocent. Nor did she believe in innocence, or morals, or some spiritual need to be above others or whatever it was. She just believed in herself. She was the only one she could count on, and sometimes not even herself. Nonetheless, she desired that sort of cleanliness. It was inherently attractive, and she had no idea why.

"Can we finish this conversation?" she said, frustration building deep in her stomach. He needed to stop changing the subject. Judy was going to be important to her from now on. Couldn't he see that?

Apparently not, for he just shrugged. "I don't think we really need to discuss it. We both know Judy ought to go to boarding school. It'll be best for her, and this way you can have the life you deserve." He gave her a tender look. "You deserve to be worshiped and put on a pedestal, Adele, not made to care for some man's brat."

Her vision narrowed, and she slapped him so hard

that his head flew back.

He sat there in shock for a full thirty seconds. She could understand that. She was shocked, too, but he couldn't call her daughter a brat. He couldn't refer to her Judy as "some man's." She was Troy's daughter, yes, but she was also Adele's. *Theirs.* Hal had better not come between her and her daughter.

"What was that about? Adele, seriously. All you all right?" His tone was confused, concerned, and innocent.

Did he not believe she was capable of natural feeling? Judy was her child. Of course she'd defend her. Adele could say horrid things about Judy, but she darn well wasn't going to let anyone else. Judy deserved better than that.

Better than me, Adele thought, but she brushed it away. That was a different discussion altogether. If she thought about that, she'd probably hurt herself, and hurting herself wasn't an option. Not when a little girl somewhere in France was counting on her to be a mother.

"Hal, don't you ever speak of my girl that way again, or we're through." Her voice sounded colder than she'd intended, but perhaps that was for the best. "I won't be sending her to boarding school, just so you know. She will be living with me. With us, if you're willing. I won't drive you off if you agree to this, but you must agree. There will be no compromises. There is no other option."

Hal blinked then laughed uneasily. "Surely you're joking? You don't want her. You've told me often what a bother having a little girl about is. Why, we were going to Italy in October, I thought. Where would we leave Judy? She's just a little girl, and she'd be better off in school, anyway."

"I ... I don't care. I want to be with her." Adele blinked, surprised by the rush of emotion which had brought on a great deal of tears. They began trickling down her cheeks inexplicably. "I don't know why I feel like this, but I do. I want her back, Hal. I ... I want her back!"

"There, there!" Hal slid his arms around her waist and pulled her close.

Adele let her head drop against his shoulder. It wasn't extremely comforting, and she was rather disgusted with him, but it was something, at least. His awkward back pats helped, even if they were a bit lacking in understanding. Soft words, laced with confusion, that meant nothing were better than nothing at all.

"Adele, are you just missing her? Just afraid that Troy will take her? Because if so, I'm perfectly willing to go to court over this. We can fight for full custody—and I'm sure there are boarding schools nearby so you could have the freedom you need and still visit her ..."

Adele sighed. He didn't understand at all. She didn't need her freedom if Judy wasn't going to be a part of it. The freedom to love who she chose was important, too, despite the fact that it might hurt. That Judy might be just as disappointing to Adele as Adele was to Mrs. Collier. That she might quarrel and hate her and tell her she was a horrid mother. And Adele would believe her. That she wasn't capable of the type of love Judy wanted.

But what did that have to do with anything? Judy was only six. A six-year-old wouldn't mind a mother who wasn't perfect. Or, at least, so far Judy hadn't seemed to mind.

Yes, she'd just keep loving on Judy and hope everything turned out for the best. She would love Judy in a quiet way—she must—and hopefully the girl would pick up on it. Judy was remarkably sensitive to others' feelings. Adele had noticed that before, and it would serve her well now.

"So you will not agree to have Judy live with us?" Adele asked.

"No, Adele." He said the words softly, but they cut right into the deepest part of her heart. "I don't think I'm the type to be a father. And when I asked you to marry me, it was with the understanding that that was what you wanted. I think perhaps you're just tired and confused, though, so I won't end things. I'm sure in time—"

"I will."

"What?"

"I will end things." She pulled away from him and stood. "I will end things with you. I don't feel a need to

143

continue our relationship if that means ruining things with my daughter. I love Judy." There. She'd said it aloud. She'd do anything for her daughter. And if that meant giving up the man who wanted the same things she did, who she was attracted to and thought she loved, that was fine.

Judy came first now. She *must* come first. Even if it hurt. Even if it was a part of her soul laid bare to the general public.

"You don't mean that." Hal stood and took her by the arm. "Let's take a moment and think about this, Adele! You can't mean to end our engagement over this. Why, we'd agreed—"

"Shut up, Hal." Adele removed the shiny ring that she'd only managed to find a few days ago. "I don't want you anymore. It's time to accept that." She held it out to him.

He stared at it in her palm for a moment then took it and tucked it into the pocket of his jacket. "I'll hold onto it until you're feeling slightly more reasonable."

"If by reasonable, you mean giving up my daughter, who is quite possibly the only person in this world who I love more than myself, well, then you'll never see me as anything but batty as a ... as a bat." She burst into a fit of sudden irrepressible giggles and dropped onto the park bench.

Hal stared at her as if she was crazy. Perhaps she was, just a little. She felt strange and light and giddy, as she'd not felt in ages and ages. Her heart soared, and she couldn't stop the laughter.

She oughtn't to laugh while she was trying to break up with her fiancé, but it couldn't be helped.

She stood. "I'll see you later, Hal. I'm walking home. Don't you follow me, dear—it's poor taste!" She giggled again and walked off in the direction of her flat.

The Lady of the Vineyard

Chapter Eleven

French Riviera

They were going to catch her. She ran harder, ducking her head, diving through the vineyard rows, but her legs were too short, and she couldn't get away.

They were going to catch her and take her back to England. She couldn't be with her daddy any more.

She wasn't sure who they were. It wasn't even her mother or Hal or anyone. It was a great darkness. At last she realized it was the imaginary headmistress of that boarding school her mother wanted to send her to, an old crone with evil eyes. Judy knew boarding schools were evil—Aunt Millie had read enough to her that she knew that.

The tears came streaming down as she ran—her chest ached with the exertion, and her legs were heavy. She tried to run faster, but it was like weights were attached to her shoes. She didn't seem to make progress—just running, running with nowhere to go.

She woke up panting. Her eyes flickered around the dark bedroom, moonlight outlining mysterious, foreign shapes. Fear gripped her, and she panicked, freezing.

They're going to take me away from Daddy.

More tears came, but she couldn't even move her hand to wipe them away. Even though tears were babyish. Even though she'd been told by her mother, over and over again, that being afraid was silly. That Judy was silly. That she was a baby and needed to grow up and face reality.

The reality was that they were going to take her away.

She managed to wrap her arms around herself, but it wasn't any good to hug oneself. It wasn't the same as having her father wrap her up tight and tell her everything would be all right.

But she couldn't walk all the way up through the dark house to her father's bedroom. It was too scary. Too dark. Too far away.

A soft sob rose from her throat, but she quickly

smothered it, hating that she must always be such a baby. She was so dreadfully scared of being taken away. She would *hate* to be taken away. She loved her father, loved spending time with him, loved the vineyard, loved Holt, loved France, loved Harrington, though he did his best to make her do otherwise.

She didn't want to leave.

But she must.

Oh, she wished she were a grownup and could make her own decisions! Grownups never had to leave if they didn't want to. In fact, sometimes grownups did leave, and they hurt when they did so.

If she were a grownup, she would leave her mother.

The thought was shocking, and it took Judy a few moments to recover from it.

If I were a grownup, I would leave my mother.

And she'd never come back. Ever.

She'd hurt her mother as she had been hurt every day.

And then Judy repented. No, she couldn't do that to Mother. She loved her too much. But at the same time, she didn't want to go home to her.

What could she do? Nothing. She would go back to her mother in August or September. But it wouldn't be going back to her mother, really. It'd be going back to boarding school. Going back to a place she'd never been before.

It wouldn't really be going back at all.

And holidays, she'd sometimes be with her father—he had promised that—but other times she'd be with her mother and Hal. And neither of them liked her as much as she liked to be liked.

She wished sometimes that they would love her a little—especially her mother, but even her soon-to-be stepfather. Not that he would ever really be her father. Judy was determined on that count. Mr. Hal wouldn't make a very good father; she was sure of that. He'd make a rather disagreeable one indeed.

Besides, she already had a father, and he was grand. He was upstairs in his bedroom asleep and probably wouldn't mind if she hopped up in bed with him until the fears passed.

Yet how to get up there? That was the question. Everything was so dreadfully dark.

Screwing up her courage, she leaped out of bed and hurried down the hall and up the stairs. To her surprise, as she knew it must be quite late as she'd had time to go to sleep and wake up again, a light was on in her father's room. She could see it shining under the door, bright and unconcerned with her fears.

That alone reassured her.

She crept up to the door and raised her hand to knock, thinking that it was probably not polite to open the door and just run into someone's room, when she heard her father's voice quite clearly say, "Judy is just fine, Lola, and will you stop worrying?"

Judy lowered her hand and waited. If her father

150

was talking about her over the phone, the best course of action was to listen in and see what he said.

She tried to do what was right, and Granny said eavesdropping wasn't right. But it couldn't be helped at times.

"I know, I know. She's a little girl, and she needs a mother's influence. Not that Adele was ever a *mother's influence*; she's done more harm than good. But I'm not keeping Judy here forever. I can't, I'm sorry to say. She goes back to her mother in late August." A pause. "No, I can't fight it. The law's on her side there, and I can't really prove that Judy won't be just as well off with her mother as with me." Another pause.

"It's impossible to prove emotional neglect, much less convince someone that that's a logical reason to take a child from her mother, and even if Judy were to stand before a judge and testify, do you think they'd consider a six-year-old's opinion? No, perhaps in half a dozen years, but not before then. But until September, Harrington and I will take good care of her. What is it— bread and water, walk her twice a day, make sure she's warm at night?" Daddy chuckled. "Yes, I know it's not funny ... Well, it kind of is, isn't it? A little?"

There was a long pause.

"I don't know. I think she's happy. She's never said or looked or acted otherwise. I don't know what either of us are going to do when she has to leave, Lola. I love her more than my own life, and I think it's going to hurt her a bit, too."

Judy nodded to herself. She *was* happy, and she *didn't* want to leave, and it *would* hurt to go. Living with Daddy and Harrington and Holt was an absolute dream come true. They spoiled and pampered her, which was always nice, but there was also a degree of love behind it that she wasn't used to.

It would be difficult to trade that out.

There was a long silence as Judy assumed Aunt Lola was talking before Daddy responded.

"Della cut off that option a long time ago, Lola. And, actually, I offered myself to her again when I picked Judy up to go to France." A pause. "She turned me down, of course." He grunted. "No, I suppose it wasn't very romantic, but I wasn't trying to be romantic, nor do I feel I should have to. Good sense should prevail.

"Oh, shut up, Lola. I don't want to think about what women want in their men. I just want the women in my life to use a bit of intelligence." He laughed. "No, I'm not talking about you, sweetheart." Now he sighed. "You're my good angel. I don't know what I'd do without my baby sister."

Judy could hear the smile in his voice as he spoke next: "That's just like you, matchmaking and matchmaking, but Lola, the match was already made and broken. I don't think there's any sort of healing available for us. I think it's over. Even if one end of the match would very much like it not to be ... Yes, yes, I would take her back. Does that make me weak? No. It doesn't. It makes me forgiving, now, doesn't it? Oh, shush. Call me whatever you will. She's my wife, and I have no moral reason to have divorced her even if the law has decreed otherwise." He hesitated. "No. If she hasn't been faithful, I don't want to know. I'm willing to forgive her for it. Besides, there's no real proof that she's ... Oh, don't give me that. I *don't* want to hear it."

He was silent for a long time. "I know, Lola. Perhaps it would be letting myself be trodden on, but I think she wouldn't come back to me unless she'd really turned a corner. Really changed. If she's changed, perhaps there's hope for her salvation. I'm the only real Christian she's ever known—save Millie, who she seems to ignore—and I never showed her true Christianity when I was with her. I can't help but blame myself." Another beat. "I know that sounds ridiculous. I love her. What can I say? I am ridiculous. Besides, it's hypothetical enough that I don't have to consider the moral implications. I'm just a dreamer; let me dream. But now, wait a minute!" His voice had a laugh to it. "Eloise, my dear, you've got me talking about myself! What a terrible person you are. Here I was calling to check on your health like a good brother, and you got me ranting about my love life." He chuckled. "Yes, I know you're a master conversation manipulator. I've been a victim more times than I can count."

Judy ignored this last bit. All she could think was, *He still loves Mother. He still loves Mother. He would still take her back. He would still take us back.*

The Lady of the Vineyard

But, of course, that could never happen. Mother would never come back to Daddy. She was too *Mother*. It broke Judy's heart, but that was just the way it was.

But if there was a chance, well—she'd listen on and see if it came up again.

"I'm glad you've recovered." Daddy's voice was soft now. "I'm glad. I know it's not going to be easy, but I believe you can get past this, Lola. If you want to look into adoption, I'll be there for you. So will Dave." He sighed. "I know, Lola. But wouldn't an adopted child be just as much your own? I know, darling. I know. It's going to be hard for you both. But open your heart a bit and see what God wants. Maybe that's His plan for you and Dave—to give a warm, loving home to a child who hasn't one. That's not a bad calling, you know, and I believe it's one you could both embrace. You just have to try a little."

Judy wanted to run into the bedroom and ask her father to get back on track—talking about her mother and how to get her to come see them. That was what mattered. If they could be a family again, anything was possible. Even if it would be a miracle.

"Yes, we can change the subject. Can't we talk about Dave and various ways to injure his body? I'm thinking poison ... No, don't hang up on me. I apologize. Gosh. You'd think you actually liked the fellow, the way you defend him, when really we both know you're just biding your time until he dies, and you can take his money ... All right, sorry! Oh, are we going

154

back there again? It's too late for that. But yes, I have thought about *that*. I want so badly to understand her. She's such an enigma, my Della. But here's what I've arrived at."

When he hesitated another beat, Judy practically bounced with impatience.

"I think it fairly killed her when her father and brothers died. She used to talk a lot about her brother Kenneth—wanted to name our son after him, though we had Judy instead. Then apparently her mother was insane with grief and said some rather hateful things to her. So Della had to go through the toughest parts of growing up without a strong male influence and with a mother who hated her. You can guess the rest. Anyway, I believe I remind her of Kenneth a little. At least, she's compared us. Did you know that? I don't think I told you. No, I don't know about that." He paused for a long moment before speaking again. Judy waited, wanting to hear more. "I'm not sure why she acted as she did after Judy was born."

She shuddered. That was one of the things that she *didn't* want to hear about. It would just be painful, to know Mother didn't love her much. Did her daddy know that what was most important wasn't what *had* happened but what *might*?

If Mother would marry Daddy again and live at the vineyard and learn to love them both, then nothing else would matter but that.

Yet Daddy continued on about things Judy was

scared to hear.

"It makes absolutely no sense to me. She was so insane after Judy was born, Lola. You weren't there, but you should have seen her. The woman could have been committed to an asylum. Manic then angry and violent—spewing hateful words, doing hateful things. I know women can act oddly after having a baby; I've heard that. But this was different. I should've done something, but I didn't know what to do. I was young, too, and inexperienced. She was falling apart, Lola, and I don't know why. I wish I did. She began to love Judy then, you know, but it wasn't enough, and she's been pushing Judy away ever since. I can't begin to understand that. Judy is my world."

That was good to hear at least.

"Yes. You're right, Lola." His voice was tired but gentle. "She is a sad, lonely woman, though she may not know it yet, and she needs Jesus desperately. He could heal her. I did try to tell Della about God a few times, but I worshiped her, and it's hard to bring up a tough subject with someone you worship. Still, I did my best."

Judy nodded. She'd heard Granny and Aunt Millie talk to Mother about God, too. It didn't do any good. Mother just about hated that Man called Jesus, even when Aunt Millie talked about Him loving and saving and protecting. All things Judy thought would make Him a good friend to have.

"No, I actually haven't spoken to Judy about it.

We pray together morning and evening, and I read her the Bible, but she seems somewhat closed off. I wish I knew why. At church? Mostly boredom. But what else is a child supposed to feel like there? I know I was ... I will keep trying, though. Don't you worry. She's a child, and a sweet one at that, and there's no reason why she shouldn't be open to our Savior's love."

Judy *was* open to it. Or, at least, she was coming to be open to it. At first, she hadn't known what to think. All her mother's teachings were so different from her daddy's, and her grandmother's were different than his, too.

Her daddy talked about grace, love, and arms held wide open. Her mother talked about restrictions, anger, and a lack of forgiveness. Her granny talked about rules, goodness, and purity. Judy wasn't sure which was right. They couldn't all be.

But, slowly, she was coming to realize that her father's was the one she wanted. It was the nicest. Her mother's lacked any loving Someone taking care of her, and Judy wanted that loving, all-powerful Someone. Her granny's didn't leave much room for little girl mistakes. Judy was always making mistakes.

But she liked her father's religion. Perhaps, someday, somehow, it could become hers. Wouldn't that be lovely?

Anyway, if nothing else, her daddy would love and protect her for now—and it would seem Aunt Lola was very much on her side, too. And maybe, someday, there would be Mother. At least, it was to be hoped for.

For now, Daddy was there to keep away the monsters—even if sometimes those monsters were in the form of her own mother. She had nothing to fear.

Judy returned to her room and soon fell asleep, dreaming of the Bible stories her father had told her, laced with wonder and miracles and truth and love.

Chapter Twelve

London, England

The night wore on, black and empty. Adele had never been one to struggle to fall asleep, but suddenly it was near impossible.

For all her brave words, giving up the life she had planned with Hal Acton set her world spinning. It wasn't so much that she missed him—in some ways she was relieved—but that the change had been sudden, and she wasn't sure what to make of the Adele who would do such a thing. To be fair, this was the first time in years that she'd voluntarily given up something she wanted just because she didn't think it was the right thing to do.

But Adele wanted Judy back. She wanted her little girl to be waiting for her when she got back from work—instead of silent nothingness. She was lonesome and not even sure why.

She pushed herself up and turned on the light. The little hand pointed to three, and she'd yet to nod off, even for a second. Neither her exhaustion or her depression were helping her sleep tonight.

Hal was only a secondary problem. Yes, his validation and affection was missed, and he did help chase the demons away. But it wasn't affecting her as strongly as she'd assumed it would. He hadn't become a permanent fixture in her life, and she was perfectly willing to leave him.

It was giving up Judy that was difficult.

Judy was Adele's life. It was hard to admit, even to herself, but it was true. Judy was her good angel, and Adele never wanted to let her go.

Especially not to Troy. Troy would take Judy so thoroughly that Adele would have no hope of winning her back. She knew that for sure. Troy was the type who could easily capture Judy's heart and whisk her away from Adele forever. Adele had been won by him, hadn't she? Far too easily, far too quickly.

That must be why we couldn't stay together, she thought. *If it was really going to last, we would have taken a bit more time. Or, at least, a decent amount of time. A few months ...*

Troy seemed the sort who knew what he wanted and went and got it. In fact, she knew he was. He always had been. But did it matter if she loved Judy more than anything else? No, unless she could tell Judy, share that love, and earn her trust back—something which she knew would be a long and difficult process—she wouldn't be Judy's mother any more.

At four o' clock, she rolled out of bed and took a bath, which did little to cleanse her soul. Then she sat in the living room, a blanket tucket about her legs although it wasn't chilly, and thought.

Adele wasn't sure how she felt about not being Judy's mother. She didn't think it had been a huge part of her identity for many years, but on the other hand, maybe it was. After all, she'd wanted to take Judy with her from France, hadn't wanted to leave her.

She went to the kitchen and made herself toast. It wasn't crunchy enough, and she threw it away after two bites. Though she'd been starving two minutes ago, she wasn't hungry. Her teapot whistled, and she poured herself a cup but left it sitting on the counter to wander into her bedroom and dress for the day.

Might as well give up on sleeping. Her thoughts weren't stopping any time soon.

She was sure that Judy loved her. Sure that she would be loyal. Wasn't she? After all, Troy had only known her a matter of weeks, and Judy was a cautious child. Judy was a sweet little thing, but she was shy, and surely her father ...

But Troy probably wasn't someone Judy would be shy with. He absolutely adored Judy, and Judy was sure to respond to that. Especially since Adele had been an insufficient mother to Judy for years and years.

After dressing, Adele went into the bathroom and looked into the mirror. She didn't recognize the woman who stared back at her.

In the last few days, she'd given up maintaining her appearance, wore whatever was at the front of her closet, and forgot about her fingernails, hair, and makeup. She never dabbed on perfume or wore heels. What was the point? She wasn't looking for a man, was she? And she had no desire to look nice for herself.

She felt bad then, and brushed a bit of powder over her cheeks, but she simply wasn't in the mood to dress up. It was close enough to seven; she'd open the shop now. She grabbed her purse and left her flat behind.

She closed her eyes and ran her hands over her face as she sat behind the counter, thinking about her mess of a life. It was overwhelming to realize that she was so awful.

How could she have given Troy up?

She wanted to make it right, but it was too late. There was no way on heaven or earth that Adele was going to go back to Troy. She would never be Judy's mother again.

She was so afraid of not being Judy's mother. Yet she couldn't be. Because, even if she could win back Judy's heart, how could she trust herself to be a good mother? How could she trust herself not to hurt Judy again? How could she trust herself not to be the kind of mother she'd been for six years? How could she ask Judy to give up the father whom she must have come to love and admire?

It was going to be a long, lonely life without Judy, though. So what could she fill her time with? She couldn't think of a thing that would actually help her get through the day.

She almost wished for a brief moment that when Troy had asked her to go with him that day that she'd gone. She loved Judy, after all, and if Troy wasn't so bad, which she didn't believe he was ... Well, what was it about Troy that made it so difficult for her to like him?

There wasn't a thing truly wrong with the man that wasn't overcome by his variety of strengths. She actually like him a great deal, in fact. At first, it had been because he was clean and good and wholesome, and a part of her had wanted that in her life. But she had soon learned that that wasn't the only thing about him she admired. He had a great sense of humor, was adorably sweet, and cared about her in a way no one else had.

He didn't want to control her. He wanted her to be his, yes, but that was only natural. He was seeking to give her more of a life, to make her happy, to give her some joy in this aching, sad world.

And yet it was impossible for her to accept his goodness. She didn't know why. Perhaps it was because he loved her so much.

The bell over the door tinkled, and Adele looked up to see her mother enter the shop. She stood there straight and stiff, glanced about her, then locked eyes with Adele.

"I haven't been by in a while, and I didn't realize you'd remodeled a bit," she said. "It's not as overdone as it had been."

Adele didn't bother to inform her mother that it was because she was waiting for a new flower shipment to arrive, which happened to be running three days late, and was running low on stock. She'd fill it to the brim with blooms as soon as she could. It might not be classy, but it'd be fragrant.

Mother cocked her head, then approached the counter at a brisk pace. She set her purse on the edge and gave her daughter a look-over.

"You look horrid," she said. "You're too thin, you have dark circles under your eyes, and your hair is a wreck."

Adele sighed heavily and stood. "Thank you." Of course her mother could never admit concern—her words came out as insults, and Adele hated it. Was she like that with Judy? Her guilt sometimes told her so.

Mother reached across the counter and took her

daughter's hand. Though Adele flinched away, she held firm. "How are you feeling?"

Adele glowered at her mother, angry at the intrusion, angry because the only reason her mother would touch her was to hold her still. To keep her from leaving. *To take control.* "I'm fine."

"You look ... ill."

Adele at last managed to draw away. "I'm not."

"Are you sure?"

"Yes. Now, what do you want?"

"I haven't heard from you in two weeks. I worried."

"There has been no need to contact you with Judy away." Adele picked up a stack of order forms and tucked them under the counter even though they didn't belong there, anything to keep her hands busy. "You haven't been around to pick her up, and she hasn't been around bothering me about calling you and arranging for you to pick her up. There was no need."

"I'm your mother. Of course there's a need!"

"There's not much of a need for anything. Did I mention that I broke my engagement with Hal?"

"Oh." Mother exhaled. "So that's it. You're moping around because of him." She frowned and folded her arms. "I always knew he would be unfaithful."

"He's not unfaithful. When I said that I broke up with Hal, I meant it. I told him I never wanted to see him again. Me, not him. He's a good man." Or, at least, as good as any other men she'd dated over the years—

maybe a bit better. She wouldn't give her mother the satisfaction of admitting that much, however.

"Why did you break up with him?"

"I wanted to."

Mother leaned back and folded her arms. "Then I don't think you have a right to act so depressed. If it was your decision—"

"I said it was my decision. I didn't say it was an easy decision. Let's just leave it at this; I broke off my engagement with Hal Acton, but I didn't do it because I wanted to. I did it because ... because ..." Adele rubbed her forehead. "I'm not really sure why I did it. I just did. Let's drop the subject. Are you leaving now?"

"I suppose I could if you want me to. You are at work after all ... and I shouldn't bother you. I just don't understand. I didn't like Mr. Acton, but I wasn't blind, and I could see that you liked him. And now this? And you don't even know why? This kind of thing has happened before, but there's always been a reason, even if it was only that you tired of the man."

"I didn't tire of Hal."

"Well, then why?"

Adele took a deep breath. "It ... it was wrong."

"Wrong?" Mother's voice rose a pitch above its usual tone.

"Wrong to take Judy away from ... To try to give her a new father when she ... Well, she was also ... Hal didn't want Judy, and I *do*, and ... I don't know why. It just was wrong."

166

"Have my words of wisdom gotten to you all of the sudden?"

"No. Well, maybe a little. It didn't help for you to be continually railing at me, always acting as if I was an adulteress of some sort."

"I believe I only said you were committing adultery once."

"Yes, but you kept implying it over and over after that."

"Well." Mother adjusted her hat. "Perhaps I did, but it's nonetheless true. You made a lifetime commitment before God and the world. A silly thing like a divorce doesn't reverse it."

"I don't quite agree with that, and I doubt Troy would, either—or Millie, for that matter, as she's never brought up that objection. But I do think that Judy isn't ready for another man in her life, and I should act on that."

"You're going back to Troy, then?" Her voice raised to what was almost an excited squeal—or as close to an excited squeal as Adele's mother could get.

Adele laughed halfheartedly. As if he'd ever take her back. "No."

"Oh." Disappointment registered on her face.

"I'm sorry ... I just can't go back to him. I was absolutely miserable with Troy. You can't possibly understand how miserable."

Mother pursed her lips. "Was he unkind to you? I wouldn't have believed it before, but a woman isn't bitter for six years for no reason."

"No." Troy had been a gentleman, even when he was furious at her, which he had often had cause to be. "He wasn't. He ... I ... we ... I just wasn't happy with him. He never loved me, not after the first few months."

"But I thought you'd decided that Judy's happiness meant more to you than your own."

"I ... I doubt I'll be seeing much of Judy any more. I think Troy's going to ask me if she can come live with him permanently."

"Are you serious? But ... her friends are here."

Adele shrugged. "She's six. She can make new friends. I doubt she'll even care. I want so badly to call that man up right now and tell him to bring my baby back—that we had a deal; that he was supposed to leave her with me—but that's not what Judy wants. She'll miss you, but she'll be happier, and Troy will bring her to visit every once in a while, I'm sure."

"So you're cutting off all ties with the daughter you claim to have given up your happiness for?" Mother arched an eyebrow. "That doesn't make any sense."

Desperation caused Adele's throat to ache again. "He's got to bring her to visit me sometime, hasn't he? He can't keep her away from me all the time."

"He can't keep her away from you at all. Judy is your daughter. Legally, he has no right to her—at least not outside of scheduled weeks. You took that right away from him."

"Judy doesn't want me. She wants him, and I won't take her away. But I will be in her life occasionally, and then she won't have to deal with the awkwardness of having two fathers. Does that make sense to you?"

"Yes, it does. Though ... Adele?"

"I'm still here."

"Why not go back to Troy?" Mother's voice was softer than it'd been in years now, and that in and of itself made Adele look up. "You're unhappy, and you might as well be unhappy with him as elsewhere. Besides, what's to say you won't find happiness with him? It's the right thing to do. You should give Judy a complete family, Adele. It's not fair to her, how she's lived her entire life only half-complete."

"I couldn't go back to him." *I'm not worthy.*

"Maybe you could if you tried. What's wrong with him? I've never seen him do or say anything that repulsed me. What did he do or say to you?"

"He's ... dull." Lies, but it made her feel just a bit better to say them. It always did.

"He's not dull! He's interesting. Much better than Hal Acton, at any rate."

Adele bristled. "Hal was fascinating."

Mother raised her shoulders ever so slightly, as if she wanted to shrug but wasn't able to compel herself to find the energy to do so. "Perhaps, but I never saw evidence of it. He seemed completely normal to me.

169

Troy ... Troy had a certain something about him. And he has a wonderful way with children."

"And older women."

She laughed. "You're just trying to distract me. Anyway, you were young then, and you found the normal things that you're doing every day now boring. You don't do anything exciting when you have the chance, Adele. At first you went to wild parties and dated men—whom I might add I didn't approve of—but you settled down. You got your 'Hal,' and you got your flat, and you took up the slack here. Maybe this is what you need. It may be dull, but it is still a change."

"Well ... well ..." Adele spluttered. "You're basing this off an untested theory. There's nothing to indicate that, should I run to Troy Kee, throw myself into his arms, and promise undying devotion from now 'til forever, that he'd take me back."

"Oh, of course he would. He's a good man." Mother tossed off Adele's objections with a wave of her hand.

"I don't want to marry him simply because he thinks it's the way an honorable gentleman would act. Now, I wish you'd stop bothering me about this, Mother!" Adele exclaimed.

Mother was silent for a moment, flummoxed. "You're intent on remaining single?"

"It seems the only course for me." *At least that way I can't hurt anyone else.*

"If you've made your decision, I know I can't sway

you. Goodbye, Adele."

"Goodbye, Mother."

Mother started toward the door then turned back. "You'll ... you'll call me if you learn anything about Judy?"

"Of course."

"Very well. I'll be hearing from you then, I suppose."

"Yes, I suppose."

The Lady of the Vineyard

Chapter Thirteen

French Riviera

Daddy and Judy strolled through the vineyard one evening, hand in hand. Despite being tired—bedtimes were forgotten—and a bit sickly—so were healthy meals—Judy was the happiest girl who'd ever walked the face of the earth.

She had her father and the loveliest little room she'd ever laid eyes on. If she had a bad dream at night, she was never afraid anymore. She'd explained to her father about the dreams, and he now let Holt sleep on the floor next to her bed, ready to jump up under the covers at a word—or escort her to Daddy's room if the dream was particularly bad.

She was never presented with spinach or broccoli or other yucky green vegetables; she was never forced to eat when she wasn't hungry. She never went to sleep when she wasn't tired. Her father told her stories and was always willing to make up "one more" if it was requested. In short, she was being lovingly spoiled rotten for the first time in her life and enjoying every minute of it.

Tonight, as they strolled through the growing grapes, they chatted about this and that—the sunset, the extra hands that would be called in for the harvest in September, the way Holt always turned in exactly three circles before he laid down at night.

When they came to a seat which looked out on the sea, they sat down. The sun was just dipping below the horizon; by turning to the west, they could see it, though the evidence of its setting was everywhere in the brilliant oranges and pinks staining sea and sky and causing deep shadows between the rows.

"It's pretty here," said Judy.

"It certainly is. It's the kind of view you want to share with someone, though. It's not a peaceful-by-yourself view."

Judy considered this for a moment, then nodded. "Yes. I guess so."

A thoughtful silence.

"Daddy?"

"What, Judy?"

"Have you ever showed this to anyone before?"

"Yes. I put the bench out here for your mother. She said it was the most beautiful sight she'd ever laid eyes on."

"Did she come out here all the time?"

"Yes. But never alone. She was the one who said it wasn't a peaceful-by-yourself view."

She tilted her head up at him. "Did she ever take me out here?"

"I ... I'm afraid I don't know that, Judy. After you were born ... your mother stayed about a month. I was in Paris for most of that time."

"You were?"

"Yes. I think ... I think that's when I lost her."

Judy's hands tightened into fists. It wasn't fair that a loved one could be lost so easily. "Why?"

"I suppose she was lonely."

"Didn't she have Holt?"

Daddy reached a hand up and rubbed the back of his neck. "She doesn't like Holt."

"Why not?"

"He was always eating things of hers. Clothing, books, family heirlooms."

Judy wrinkled her nose. "I guess if he ate my things, I wouldn't like him either."

"Then you'd best not keep your things in piles on the floor." Daddy shifted on the bench. "That was your mother's habit."

"Mother says it makes finding what she needs easier."

"I think, rather, that it makes you step on things and break them. Or trip on them and break you."

Judy laughed. "I guess so."

"That was another thing that annoyed her. I was forever picking up her things and putting them away."

Judy shook her head. "She doesn't like that at all! You should hear her when Granny does it."

"I imagine she throws a first-rate fit."

"Yes."

A moment of silence.

"Judy?"

"Yes, Daddy?"

"I don't have a chance with her." His face was long and his eyes squishy-looking. Judy understood the feeling. Too much sadness in her heart to even cry but feeling like it all the same.

"I guess not. But I don't either."

He glanced down at her. "Oh, I don't know, Judy. You might find her changed. She'll have been missing you."

"But I won't go back." Judy forced the word through her clenched teeth. "I won't." She couldn't. She loved her father now, and it would break her heart and rend her soul to leave him. She couldn't go back to her mother's neglect. Couldn't hear that she was a bother again. Not after she'd been loved.

"We'll see. I might be able to get the court order

176

changed so she has no choice."

"Soon?"

"She promised you could stay with me until the end of the summer. We'll figure things out this fall."

"Like school? I have to go to school this year."

"There's a perfectly good school nearby. Granted, it's Catholic, and I'm Protestant, but I'm sure the nuns at St. Albertine's would be perfectly willing to take you anyway. You can always be taught the good from the bad at home."

"What's Catholic and Protestant?"

"They're religions, baby." Daddy squeezed her shoulder. "It's a bit difficult to explain, but I'll try. Basically, Catholics were the old Christians, from many years ago, and then Protestants are the people who decided the old Christians were corrupt—at least back then—and changed things. Then the Catholics also changed, too. But they started being two separate churches."

"So we're Protestant?"

"Mmhmm. We're Church of England, actually, if only because that's the church I went to as a boy."

"Okay." Judy didn't quite understand the difference still, but she was sure he could explain it better later. She could sort out her father's religion better now, though. It was more than heroic stories, she realized; it was about Someone loving her no matter what. It was something real and here and now, something she wanted to become a part of. As she was beginning to learn a bit of French, soon she'd be able to understand what was being said at church without her father whispering a translation into her ear. She felt that would help her greatly, too.

All in all, she wanted to know a lot more about that Man, Jesus. Anyone who stood for love was worth getting to know better, as far as she was concerned.

Chapter Fourteen

London, England

Adele rifled through boxes of toys and clothes in Judy's bedroom, searching for her diamond earrings.

Due to her house-cleaning, or rather, the lack of it, things tended to drift about in her flat. What started in the living room might mysteriously end up in the bathroom. She didn't know how it happened. It just did.

She found one in a box of doll clothes—*what on earth?*—and, having dug through every one of Judy's possessions, left the room. There. She'd searched the entire flat. Chances were, she'd dropped it somewhere—at work or at Millie's.

Or she'd lost it in the street and would never see it again. What a dismal prospect. After she'd been trying to pick herself up and look her best, too.

"Where, oh where, has my diamond earring gone?" She sang the words loudly and somewhat off-pitch to herself as she put the found one in her jewelry box which rested on the kitchen counter. "Where, oh where can it be? Oh, bother. I'd lose my head if it weren't attached to my shoulders. Now I've nowhere else to look, and those were a present from ... someone."

She wondered vaguely if her inability to remember the names of past boyfriends and beaux was a symptom of this whole giving up on men thing. She supposed it could also be due to having drank too much most of the time she was dating them. Whatever the reason, she wanted to forget anyway.

She walked into her room and opened the door of her closet. A landslide of various objects fell out, nearly smothering her.

"For the thousandth time, Adele Collier, don't open the closet door or you'll get crushed!" she muttered to herself, kicking aside boxes, clothing, and other random objects. "Perhaps Troy had a point with that 'straightening-up' obsession of his. At least his belongings aren't smothering him."

She was talking to herself again. She'd been doing

that an awful lot lately. But she couldn't help it. There wasn't anyone to talk to but herself.

Adele began scooping up the mess, throwing clothes into one pile, random papers into another pile, purses into another, and so on. At the very back of the closet, underneath dresses, coats, and hats years out of style that she'd saved for unknown reasons, she found a small hat box with a note pinned to the ribbon tied around it.

She bit her lip as memories rushed back to her. Christmas morning, 1931. Joy and laughter and mistletoe. Harrington frowning grumpily at their antics, secretly delighted. Had Lola been there? Her mother? Millie, even? She wasn't sure, but she believed so.

She only remembered *him* with his messy strawberry blonde hair, his sparkling blue eyes, that mustache that irritated her to no end.

"How could I be so happy when I was going to have a baby?" Adele murmured. "I ... I didn't want that baby, but I was still happy. I was just ... glad to be with him. Even if I thought the circumstances were inconvenient. Even if I didn't understand how important that baby was going to be to me."

The wonder of this struck Adele in a whole new light. Happy? To be with him? She must have been a very different woman at the time.

"Of course I was," Adele said. "I was in love with him; in spite of it all, I was in love with him and determined to be his wife regardless of the unwanted child. I must have been a very different woman indeed. Wasn't I?"

Have I changed? Other than learning the average things everyone does over the years—like never let your best friend do your hair, no matter how badly she wants to—have I changed? I must have. I must have changed.

She slipped the ribbon off the box and examined the note tied to the outside. It was written in her own handwriting.

"Remember to burn it as soon as he signs those papers. Or wait until Judy's a little older and tell her why."

Venomous words, dashed off boldly, angrily. Adele sighed. *See, I have changed. Back then I wasn't smart enough to realize that I never remember my notes.* She slowly opened the box and reached inside, pulling out a bundle of notes and photographs. She unfolded one scrap of paper and read it.

Left early today. Didn't want to wake you up. As I said last night, I'll be in Paris for a week. I'll call this afternoon or this morning if I can't wait. Be safe. I love you.

Troy

Adele dropped the note back into the box. "Granted, he could be sweet when he wanted to be. But that doesn't change anything. He's still ... still ... Well, whatever he is, I won't go back to him."

She shifted through the notes and letters, reading some. The photographs she examined—pictures of Troy and herself, of the vineyard, occasionally even one of a very small Judy. Oh, right, they'd had a few snapshots of her taken in the first week.

She sighed and stuffed them back into the box. As she did so, she dropped a sealed envelope; it drifted across the floor when she placed the box on the top shelf of the closet. She turned, caught sight of a flash of white, and picked it up. The unopened envelope was addressed to her.

Slitting it open, she pulled out a sheet of paper and unfolded it.

Dear Della,

I promised to write from Paris before our fight, so that's what I'm doing. I would call, but it's late, and the only times I have free are late at the moment.

So this is me telling you that I miss you so much that it hurts.

Is Judy all right? I miss her so much! Are her eyes darkening? I have mixed feelings about the color they take on. I want her to have my eyes, but I'd rather she have yours.

I know, I know. You've always said you wished

you had blue eyes. They're a lot more romantic—blue skies and oceans and violets, et cetera.

But, you know, brown eyes have their advantages, too. For one thing, they're more sun-resistant. Also, chocolate. Besides, I think it's easier to fall into brown eyes. Such has been my experience.

Nonetheless, I may be able to love her if she resembles me. Or my sister. Lola called the other day and mentioned that she thought Judy is her mirror image from the photo we sent, which would please her immensely.

But I'm off-subject now. I've been thinking lately about our fight. Perhaps you're right. I have been spending a lot of time away from you recently.

But I thought you understood. You know how things are going to be. Children cost money. And not just food and clothing ... what about ponies and puppies and a trip to wherever she wants? And college? I want Judy to have all those things.

Besides, Della, even if you don't know it, times are hard. I'm having a difficult time keeping our heads above water. I wish you'd try to understand that.

I know you're used to getting what you want when you want it, but that can't always happen. I wish I could make it happen—that's what I'm trying to do—but I can't. I'm not all-powerful.

So you've got to tell me how to make this right. I don't know how ... but I'm willing to try anything to restore your faith in me.

In closing, I can only say that I love you, and I'll crawl back on my knees if I have to. So forgive me, and when I get home, I'll stay, and if I have to leave again, I'll take you and Judy with me. We'll have a second honeymoon. It'll be fun.

With all the love in my heart,

Troy

Adele pulled her knees up to her chest. *Serves me right for not opening my mail. Too busy packing my bags to read it. Idiot.* She dropped her head on her knees and tried to stave back the tears.

I left him. A few quarrels, and I left him. But it wasn't his fault. It was mine. I was the one who couldn't stand the responsibility, the self-denial ... I was the one who was emotionally and physically unbalanced, sick at heart. He was trying to be supportive.

She'd left him, taken the baby he adored, and removed his rights to see her. And then she hadn't even taken proper care of Judy. Not really.

I've put him through hell, and he hasn't given up on me—not until now, anyway. He asked me to come with him, and like an idiot I had to refuse. And I've lost my last chance. I've lost him.

Oh, Troy. Could you ever forgive me?

Chapter Fifteen

French Riviera

Daddy tucked the covers cozily around Judy and kissed her forehead. "Now you're really going to have to go to bed, all right? It's time to sleep, and I mean it. We're going to have regular bedtimes from now on."

Judy wiggled and then sat upright, brushing the covers back. She wasn't tired yet. At least, not tired enough to sleep. "Just one more story! Tell me about when Aunt Lola threw *Hard Times* at you again."

Daddy chuckled but gently pressed her back into the bed. "I will not! You're going to sleep. You have dark circles under your eyes, baby. You're my little girl, and my little girl has rosy cheeks and a spring in her step."

Judy pouted, sticking out her lip as far as it would go. It was a new skill she'd acquired in the last few weeks. "I don't want to sleep. Oh, just one more story, Daddy! Tell me ... tell me about when you met Mother." This was something Judy had always wanted to know about but never had the courage to ask. However, she was starting to get to know her father a lot better, and this gave her the courage to ask questions. Besides, it was only fair that she should know. After all, she'd come because they'd met, hadn't she? At least, she thought that was how it worked.

Daddy winced. "I really think you ought to get a good night's rest, baby."

"It won't take long, will it? Just tell me how you met her. I've always wanted to know. Please, Daddy? Please?"

Daddy sighed. "Oh, all right. But you have to lie down and rest, and I'll turn off the light while I tell it. Okay?"

"Okay," Judy agreed.

He rose and flicked off the light before returning to her bedside where he tucked the covers securely about her for the third time that night. "Now let me see. Once upon a time—"

"But it's a real story, isn't it?"

He grinned. "Oh, all stories happened 'once upon

a time,' even if they're real. They must, for even pretend stories should have a thread of truth in them. If they don't, they're no good."

"Do you think Cinderella really could have happened, then?"

"Perhaps, perhaps." He held his arms out to her, his silhouette visible in the moonlight coming from the window. Judy glady crawled into his lap and laid her head against his chest. "Now, where was I?"

"Once upon a time ..."

"There was a young man. He lived in a vineyard in France. His sister had gotten married the year before, so he was alone. He had a friend named Harrington, but Harrington wasn't the best of company. Harrington had a tendency to spend most of his time in his room, leaving the young man alone. So he missed his sister."

"Aunt Lola?"

He shifted so his back was propped up against the headrest. "Her name was Eloise, but she went by that undignified moniker, yes."

"The young man's name was Troy," Judy whispered, smiling.

"I guess so." He took her hand and squeezed it briefly. "Now, for his sister's birthday, Troy went one bright spring day to London, where his sister lived with the infamous Mr. Cole."

"Uncle Dave?"

"Yes. Now, no more interrupting." He gently tapped the tip of her nose with his fingertip.

"All right."

"Where was I?"

"He went to London for his sister's birthday."

"Oh, right. The sister, Lola, and her husband, Dave, were the most sickening pair of lovebirds the man had ever come across. They drove him crazy, and he couldn't stay with them for long periods of time. So he went on a walk."

"That's when you met Mother?"

"Not exactly. I was walking past a little flower shop, happened to glance in the window, and just stopped in my tracks. You know what I thought?"

"What?"

"'That,' I said to myself—" Daddy's voice was oddly tight. "—'is the most beautiful woman I've ever seen in my life.'"

"Really? Just like that?"

"Just like that. Now it's time for bed." He rose with her still in his arms then tucked her back under the covers.

She grabbed his sleeve and tugged. "But, Daddy, you haven't even been properly introduced!"

"Oh, well, can't that wait for another night?"

"No, Daddy, please?"

He knelt beside the bed to continue the story. "I walked into the shop, and I ordered a bouquet for Aunt Lola and another to her specifications for an unknown lady. And before I left, I made her promise to meet me there after closing time."

"Do you think she thought you were handsome?"

"I don't know. Perhaps. Or maybe she just thought it'd be a fun adventure to go out with a man she'd just met."

"That does sound like her," Judy agreed. "So you went on a date?"

"Yes. I gave her the second bouquet I bought."

Judy laughed. "You did?"

"I did."

"Did she think that was funny?"

"She thought it was very funny."

"But how did you know when you bought them that you'd be taking her out?"

"Now, she asked me the same question. I just said I didn't know for sure, but I thought it was worth the risk."

"Mother liked that, I guess?" Judy said. Her mother was the type who liked things that made no sense, like assuming someone would go out with you when she might not.

One side of his mouth tipped up at the side. "She did."

"And how long after that did you get married?"

"About ... oh, two weeks."

"That's fast!" Even Judy knew that marriage was an important step, and choosing the right person was therefore vital, which took time. Aunt Millie had told her that—it was why she didn't have a husband.

"Well, what's the use of waiting when you're

sure—or willing to take the risk," Daddy said. "I took a risk, and it didn't pay off."

Judy's chest tightened. That was awfully sad to think about.

"But don't worry about it, baby. Perhaps it did pay off. I've got you, after all, haven't I?" He took her hand and squeezed it.

Warmth rushed back into her belly, and she nodded. "Yes."

"And as long as I'm able to keep you, Judy, it doesn't matter much anymore if I made a mistake, because good came out of it. Trust me on this—it's Biblical."

"Biblical?"

"Yes. That means it's from the Bible, and you can trust the Bible. It's always true, no matter what. Remember the story about Joseph and his coat of many colors and the brothers who sold him into slavery?"

"Yes."

"Even though Joseph was badly treated by his brothers, he ended up being second-in-command to the Pharaoh. That's rather good, if you ask me. You see, stories always have a good ending, even if they start out wrong. That's the way God made the world—with happy endings."

"I guess so," Judy said, still not managing to make the connection.

"What I mean is, Judy, even if your mother hurt me—and even if I hurt her—I still have you, and I'd

192

rather concentrate on that than anything else. Wouldn't you?"

Judy grinned. "Yes."

"Good." Daddy kissed her forehead. "Now, it really is time for bed. Will you pray?"

He asked her every night, but so far Judy hadn't exactly been able to say yes. Sometimes she prayed quietly in her heart, but so far, it hadn't felt right to pray like Daddy did, out in the open and aloud. Still, perhaps she could give it a try. That didn't seem like something she could ruin too badly. "All right," she whispered, "if you'll tell me how."

"I'm glad you're ready." His voice was gravely again. "But it doesn't have to be special, Judy. Praying is just telling God about the things that worry us, and asking for Him to help, and knowing that He will."

Judy cocked her head. "He will?" No one else helped her all the time.

"Yes. Always. Sometimes He doesn't give us the answer we want, but He always gives us the answer we need. You can pray quietly in your heart, or you can pray out loud right now. Either way. Okay?"

"Okay." Judy bit her lip and closed her eyes, thinking. "Dear ... dear God?"

Was that right? She opened one eye to find her father waiting for her to continue. He nodded encouragingly, and she closed her eyes again.

"Dear God, I guess I don't know what to say, but I have a few things to ask. But maybe I'd better say thank you first. Remember, this is Judy ... Judith Ann Kee. I'm from London, but I'm in France now."

"He knows where you are, baby."

"Oh." Judy screwed up her face. "I asked for Daddy to love me a lot, and he does, so thank you. Thank you very much. That was just what I wanted."

She felt her father shift beside her, but he didn't move away, and Judy continued.

"I didn't believe in You exactly—well, Mother didn't, at least—for a long time, so I think it's awfully nice of You to answer my prayers anyway. I wouldn't have talked to someone who didn't even believe *I* existed. But I do have something else to ask. When I go back to England, I don't want to go to a boarding school away from everyone. So could I stay in France instead? I could go to school here, and Mother wouldn't mind. She doesn't love me anyway." Judy opened her eyes. "I'm all done."

"Say 'In Jesus' name I pray, amen.'"

"In Jesus' name I pray, amen," Judy echoed. "Was that all right?"

"That was fine." Daddy kissed her forehead again and stood. "You know, Judy, even though we prayed about it, you might ... you might have to go back to England. I'll come and see you as often as I can, but it's still going to be a long time until your next holiday. It won't be easy."

"I know," Judy said. "I don't expect Him to answer that one. It's too much, I suppose. I wonder if ..."

"What?"

"Could Mother come here and live with us?"

Daddy was silent for a long time, and Judy began to wonder if he'd heard her.

"Daddy?"

"No. I'm so sorry, Judy. I asked her to come, but she wouldn't. I ... I think we're ... we're just too far apart now. She doesn't love me anymore. I wish, well, it doesn't matter what I wish because she would never come."

"But if she would, you would let her?" Judy pressed. She knew Daddy still loved Mother, so maybe, just maybe ...

"Judy, it doesn't matter. I don't want to turn you against your mother; she's an adult, and she's made different decisions than I would have—than I wanted her to. And she is your mother." Daddy leaned forward to give Judy a hug. "It's going to be okay. We'll figure it out."

"But if she *would*?"

He sighed. "Yes."

"Even if she didn't love you very much?" Judy pressed.

Daddy chuckled, but it wasn't a happy chuckle exactly. "I doubt she'll ever care for me again, but that's quite all right. It was a long time ago when she loved me, and even then it wasn't exactly real. But she's going to marry this Hal Acton fellow this September, and after that, even if she did learn to care for me, I'd have to say no."

Judy stuck out her lower lip. "Why?"

"You'll understand better when you're older, but once she's married to someone else, I can't take her back." He shook his head. "It's already too much, but I could give her grace and time, if she'd just ... be a little less stubborn."

Judy scowled. If her mother being less stubborn was the requirement for her parents to live together, it would never happen. "I guess that's too much, then? To ask God to have a mommy and daddy together, not just Mother and then you in different places?"

She heard him sigh aloud. "You could ask, Judy, but ... I wouldn't bet on it. I would be surprised if your mother even speaks to me within the next few months, let alone agrees to marry me."

"Okay." Judy had to fight back the tears, but she managed to do it pretty well. None slid past her eyes. She had enough experience to keep them back. "Good night, then."

Her father's voice was still sad-sounding as he left the room. "Good night, Judy. Sweet dreams."

The next morning, Daddy and Judy drove down to town to have lunch in a little café off the beach.

Judy adored going there. She was in love with the

little cakes, or whatever they were, and she wasn't sure what to think about coffee, but it was good if she put enough milk and sugar in it—which Daddy let her do, of course.

Anyway, she was glad that she could spend this day with her father, doing quiet sorts of things. They'd decided to go down to the beach and play in the sand after lunch, which Judy loved. Making sand castles was the most fun in the world.

However, she was also unsure if she should get in the water. She'd never swam before, and the crashing waves terrified her. She supposed she'd have to ask her father to teach her some time, but right now, she didn't feel that she could even get near them. They were too drown-y.

"Did we remember your bathing suit?" Daddy asked. "We can get you changed in the restroom if you want."

Judy shrugged. "I don't think I'll need it."

"Ah, come on, Judy." Daddy winked at her. "Let's see if we can't go out a bit. I'll hold you, and you can just dip your feet in the water. It'll be all right. I promise. Trust me."

Judy wanted to trust him, but it was so difficult when she knew very well that it would be hard for her to even touch the water. It was warm, at least, not cold. She hated the cold.

Her father would be there, and she trusted him with her life. He would take care of her, and she'd hold on tight.

"Okay," Judy said. "I guess it's a good idea. But only if you'll hold me."

"Of course I'll hold you!" Daddy exclaimed. He gave her a big hug, and they went to the car to grab her bathing suit and cover.

In no time, they were at the beach ready to do what they needed to do to get in the water ... and that meant Judy staring at the crashing waves for about fifteen minutes, screwing her courage.

"We could make a sandcastle first," Daddy suggested. "Maybe it'll be easier to just sit here for a bit."

Judy swallowed. "We could try at least, but I don't think it'll be easy for me, Daddy. You see, I've never been swimming ... I never left London. All the times Mother went down to Kent, she wouldn't take me, so I know she's gone swimming probably, in the country, but I haven't. I don't like baths."

Daddy chuckled. "Yes, you do."

"Yes, but I don't like to fill them up all the way." Judy wrinkled her nose. "It's just too full!"

Daddy smiled. "I know. It's okay for you to feel that way, too, honey. It's okay for you to feel scared! But the thing is to overcome your fears. To get beyond them no matter how hard it is."

Judy took a deep breath and nodded. "You're right, Daddy. I'll try my best, really I will."

"Good girl."

He took her by the hand, and they walked toward the water. Judy closed her eyes and took a deep breath of the warm, salty air. The soft wind blowing up from the sea brushed against her cheeks, and she leaned into it.

"You're going to be all right." He squeezed her shoulder. "Don't worry, baby. I'm here. I promise."

Judy shuddered. "What if Mother comes for me?"

She heard his footsteps on the bare sand come to a stop, and he pulled her close, hand pressed to the back of her head. "Don't worry about that. I won't let her take you from me. Not now. I love you too much. You're my little sweetheart! You have to know that." He sighed. "So don't you worry about your mother. Just worry about the things at hand."

Judy pushed back and looked up at him. "I'm not as afraid of the water as I am of Mother, Daddy." Her mother held the power of life and death over her.

Her mother could make her life a terrible place, with no love, with no family, at a boarding school. Her mother could force her to accept another man as her father—when all she wanted was her own Daddy.

"Then pretend your mother is behind you and walk into the water." Daddy winked.

Judy couldn't believe he was teasing her just now, but she wiped a bare arm over her face and walked on toward the water with him at her side.

The waves rushed forward, and Judy stumbled back, but her father caught her up and held her above it as it rushed over his toes. He smiled and lowered her down, still holding her about the waist, until her tiptoes barely brushed the foamy surf.

"See? Doesn't that feel good?"

It did feel good—cool and bubbly and salty. She giggled and lowered her feet down until they touched the wet, heavy sand and sunk in. She glanced up at him, not sure what to think of the sinking, and lifted one foot. She clung to his arm for balance.

He chuckled. "Don't worry, baby. It's all right. Don't you like the way your toes sink in? You're not going to get hurt here, you know, so don't worry. Let's go out a little further. Where it's more than leftover surf."

Judy shuddered. "No."

"Oh, but we're not going to let it touch us. We'll race it. Come on." He picked her up and swung her onto his back. "Let's go."

With big strides, he walked until the waves were rocking against his knees. She buried her face in his neck and held on so tight that he was obligated to tell her to ease up a bit.

"Don't worry; I wouldn't let you get hurt."

Judy nodded, but it was hard to believe it when the waves crashed so big, and he kept walking out to meet them. She wondered vaguely if he were just a bit crazy, which she thought might be entirely possible, but at the same time, even if he were crazy, would he let her be hurt? No, he wouldn't. He loved her. He'd take good care of her. She was absolutely sure of it.

However, she had to ask. "What are we doing?"

"Playing a favorite game of mine." He hitched her higher on his back. "Your aunt Lola and I used to do this for hours. You see, you can find fun in just about anything, but waves are one of the biggest things, baby." He chuckled. "Waves, you see, will chase you!"

"Chase us!" In Judy's mind, though, that started to make sense. Waves were definitely quite evil, and they seemed the type to pursue, laughing at your slowness—to overtake and soak and drown! However, he'd called it fun and a game. How silly. That would be terrifying!

"Yes, chase us. Hold on tight now, and look! See that big wave there? Do you want it to soak us?" He pointed to a big wave cresting a few yards ahead of them.

Judy shrieked and dug her fingers into her father's shoulders. "Run, Daddy, run!"

He wheeled and raced back to the beach, the wave at their heels. They just beat it, and he turned to face the defeated lapping remains as it crested against the white sand.

"See how much fun that is?"

Judy stared at the back of his head. That wasn't fun at all! He let her slip off his back, and she could see he was laughing.

"It's not funny, Daddy," she said with dignity.

But Daddy seemed to think it was funny—or at

least he was very amused, to say the least, based on the way his chest rose and fell with chuckles and guffaws and the way his face threatened to split in two with a big grin.

"I enjoyed it, actually, Judy," he said. "I think we should do it again! Only this time, you can run beside me. Come on—let's see if you don't like it, baby! You never know until you try."

Judy hesitated. What if the wave caught her? What if she wasn't safe? What if something terrible happened? She was awash with worries. However, she did trust her father—didn't she? Did trust him to take care of her, even where water and waves came into play. She wanted to trust him, at least. Believed she could.

"Okay," said Judy, and she took his hand and let him lead her out against the buffeting waves again. This time they didn't go out quite so far, only about up to Judy's knees. The water barely lapped against her father's shins.

Tentatively, Judy glanced up at him, then took a deep breath. A wave brushed against her thighs, and she started back, but he held her there.

"Wait for a big one, baby." He squinted at the incoming waves. "That one's too small—and that one's barely a ripple. We want one that breaks just as it's coming to us." At last, a big wave came cresting toward them, spitting white foam, and her father grinned. "That's it! Ready ... set ..." He waited until the wave was almost to them then shouted: "Run, Judy, run!"

They streaked back toward the shore, Daddy matching his steps to Judy's small ones. She knew he was running slowly for her, but she simply couldn't go any faster. She only hoped it wouldn't catch her.

At last, she had beat it, and she looked back to see the big wave ebbing about her ankles, brought to nothing. She couldn't help it then—she giggled, then glanced up at her father's joyful face and laughed aloud.

"We won!"

"Yes, we did!" He scooped her up and gave her a kiss. "Want to do it again?"

"Yes, of course!" This was the best game she'd played in a long time, after all!

The Lady of the Vineyard

Chapter Sixteen

English Channel

Adele wasn't exactly sure how she got to her feet after reading that letter from Troy, let alone how she ended up standing on the deck of a boat crossing the English Channel.

She only knew that something had pushed her onward, making her keep moving when she'd rather have spent the rest of the day curled up in bed, crying.

The sea mist in her face was a stark reminder that reality was happening now. There was a battle coming up—and she was fairly sure she was going to lose it.

Even so, she must see Judy again. She wasn't quite sure about the custody rules for the parent who had primary custody visiting the other parent during their holiday, but she was sure it wasn't one in her favor.

Adele swallowed. She must believe Troy wouldn't turn her away. He couldn't be that cruel.

She had to try, and if she couldn't heal, she must suffer. Still, there was a chance—a slim chance—that Judy would choose *her*.

All Adele wanted was to see that Judy was all right, and then she'd leave and give them their space for a nice holiday. She also wanted to tell Judy about her break-up with Hal Acton in person.

It didn't seem like news to communicate over the phone.

She didn't want Judy to know she was coming, either. She wanted her daughter's unprepared reaction, the natural one, before Troy had the ability to school her—whether that was in her favor or against it.

She wanted honesty, and from a little girl like Judy, it wouldn't be hard—unless an adult like Troy told her to be polite—or told her that her mother was a wicked, selfish brat to be spurned.

But she couldn't think that of Troy. She knew he wouldn't advise Judy to hate her own mother. At least, not intentionally. It was possible his bitterness might affect the child somewhat but not enough.

No, it was unwanted positivity she had to be wary

of. That was what could ruin her chances at really knowing how her daughter felt … and, of course, really knowing how to fix the problems, whatever they were.

So with Judy's face in her heart, she marched off the boat, and with Judy's name on her lips, she caught the first train to the Riviera.

Something else was driving her besides love and devotion for her daughter. It was as if, suddenly, a little voice she'd smothered and overrode for ages somehow found its place in her mind again and began shouting in her ear.

Telling her that her actions were wrong. Telling her that she needed to go to her daughter. Telling her that Troy would let her see Judy, that Judy needed to see her mother, telling her … telling her …

No, she wasn't quite sure what all it was telling her, only that she needed to go to the vineyard. She needed to see Judy.

Troy leaned forward in the chair at his desk, rubbing his forehead. He had an impulse to slam the receiver down and end the conversation with an annoying client, but things had been a little tight of late, and he didn't dare. Especially not since Judy was his responsibility now. Especially not since every bit of money he made was going to go toward her happiness.

The Lady of the Vineyard

"I don't have a choice in the matter, Pierre!" He said the words firmly, but in truth he'd been neglecting business slightly in the last few days to be with Judy. But his customer didn't need to know that, and he wasn't going to tell him.

"*Oui*. I know that the shipment was late, but —"

The customer cut him off, his French getting increasingly accented. Troy was glad he was a native speaker—in a way, anyway. He wasn't a native, but his mother had been.

"*Non*, I'm not just making excuses! ... Nothing like that. The weather has been off. A little too warm."

Pierre informed him that he didn't care about the weather, using several expletives Troy would not be teaching Judy in their French lessons.

"I'll start with the—*oui*, first thing tomorrow, I promise ... I do know that you supply many fine establishments throughout Paris. *Non*, you won't have to move to a different supplier. I'll just ... *Oui* ... *Oui*, Pierre ... I will. Good-bye."

"What were you talking about?" Judy looked up from the chessboard which she and her doll, Marilou, were playing with.

"Just arguing with a customer." Troy stood and stretched. "Tomorrow is going to be a busy day, but I refuse to work on a Sunday, even after church. So what do you want to do this afternoon? I'm yours."

"We could—" Judy began, but the sound of a car coming up the driveway, and Holt's violent barking, brought her to a stop.

"I wonder who that could be?" Troy mused, walking to the window. "A cab." He stepped back. "Stay here. I'll be back in a moment."

Adele's feeling upon seeing the house again could only be described as wonder. It had not changed in six years.

Same wide six steps; same big double doors looking awkward in the small frame of the house; same ugly brass door-knocker; same second story balcony hanging off the west side giving the house a lopsided look. Even the same little metal table and chairs in the corner of the veranda.

All the same. All forcing the word 'charming' into her head despite their gangly awkwardness. Like Troy, she supposed. At least, it reminded her of Troy in a way.

Of course, a lot of this house was going to remind her of Troy simply because this was where she had been with him, as his wife, for almost a year. Where she'd brought Judy home to.

So many memories. Not all of them bad, as she'd originally thought. Some of them were good, grand in fact, and led her to reminisce.

She paid the cabman and watched him drive off

between the vineyard rows. She'd always thought it funny how the grapes came right up to the house, with no space for a formal yard save the little garden in the back which had deteriorated over the years. But, she supposed, that was part of its charm.

That dog—Holt—was still here. He was barking but hadn't come down from the veranda. She stayed where she was, hoping he'd settle down enough to let her walk into the house. He'd never cared for her, and she wasn't taking any risks.

Hearing the door open, she turned to face her ex-husband. His eyes gave him away. Despite a stoic face, he appeared to be struggling for composure. She supposed this must be quite the shock for him. She didn't blame him. It was a shock for her.

Yet she'd had to come. Her soul, her conscience, her love for Judy required it.

"Lie down, Holt."

For once, the big yellow dog obeyed. Adele understood. Troy's tone was all "don't test me" with no wiggle room.

"Troy," she said, smiling tentatively. She took a step or two toward him, held her hand out. She was willing to shake his hand if he were willing to shake hers. But he didn't even glance at her hand; his eyes were glued to her face, and he seemed unwilling to make any movement.

Perhaps he was afraid she'd disappear. Well, really, she wasn't here for him, but—a part of her wondered ... a part of her was curious, she supposed she ought to say. Wanted to know what the possibilities for them were. Wanted to know if maybe, just maybe, he was open to the idea of a relationship.

It was a long shot, but after she'd settled things with Judy, she might try to rekindle the romance. Just a bit. She was willing to let him in, though he'd have to make at least a few tentative steps toward her.

Yet pride wasn't an issue anymore. When she'd come here, she'd given up pride. At least, she felt she had; she wasn't going to base her decisions on it. She could humble herself to make Judy happy, and to see if a relationship with him was possible.

"Della. What are you ... what are you doing here?" he asked, stuttering slightly.

Not quite the reaction she'd been looking for, at least as far as his words and manner, but that stutter, and the wild churning of his mind that she could see reflected in his confused blue eyes, were in her favor.

At least, she believed they were. But that was something to worry about later. Just then, everything regarding anybody, including Troy, was something to worry about later, after she was sure of Judy. Judy needed to come first. Still, she couldn't help making a slightly flirtatious reply.

She smiled. "You barged in on me last month, so I'm barging in on you. Seems only fair."

Troy cocked his head to the side, a slight smile quirking up one side of his lips as he considered this. "I guess."

"You sound like Judy." If she remembered correctly, "I guess" was one of her favorite phrases. Now, as Troy took a bit to respond, apparently mulling her very simple words about in his brain as if she were some philosopher, she thought about that.

"I guess" was a rather unsure little phrase. Lacking in confidence. She wondered vaguely if she'd done that to her daughter—made her unsure of her standing with her mother, and therefore with the world.

She'd heard little girls—as well as little boys—had a unique attachment with their mother. Her mother had been unloving and hateful, and this had made Adele hard and bitter.

But, perhaps, some girls reacted quite the opposite. With meekness. With fear. Losing confidence, wilting under their mother's neglect and unconcern for their welfare.

She only hoped that a little girl could recover from such a thing if she were given the right amount of love, care, and reassurance.

The corner of Troy's mouth quirked up then. "I guess," he repeated, smothering a smile. She could tell he was amused with himself; he was often amused with himself. It was one of the most adorable things about him, honestly.

Adele raised her eyebrows and nodded toward the house behind him. "May I come in?" It was just like him to forget to invite her, and today he seemed even more distracted than usual.

"I ... I ... I guess." He flushed until his ears turned red, whirled around and marched through the door, leaving it open for her.

She followed, entering for the first time in years. She wondered at his befuddlement, even if he was somewhat surprised to see her. He had seemed so cocky when he came for Judy last month. Well, to be fair, she *had* caught him off-guard. But it seemed more than that.

As if her presence, unannounced, had affected him. Yes, she did wonder.

He led her into his little office which was truly a parlor. The room sported a sofa, two chairs, cabinets full of books and odds-and-ends, and his desk with its neatly-stacked piles of paper.

It was just the way she remembered, with its mahogany and white color scheme and its cozy but neat look. Masculine yet classy. Not cluttered at all despite the various random things he had scattered about. Everything was convenient but also quite neat.

She glanced about the room and her eyes landed on her girl, still blessedly unaware of her presence as she played with a chessboard. It was an old one with hand-carved figures, and Troy had owned it when Adele lived there.

Judy looked happy. Her hair was a bit of a mess, unbraided and lacking its usual ribbon. She was wearing saddle shoes without socks, and her dress had a big red-colored stain which Adele could imagine being some sort of jam—it also lined the edges of her lips and a peculiar spot stood out above her left eyebrow.

But she was still Judy, Adele's precious, beautiful Judy.

Chapter Seventeen

"Hello, Judy." It was as if Adele's eyes saw her for the first time. A precious, lonely little girl, every movement soft and methodical, her gentleness and sensitivity so apparent in even her quiet play. Her daughter. Her love.

Judy started and sat up, bumping the chessboard which in turn bumped Marilou, sending her sprawling on her back with her skirts flying every which way.

The child visibly swallowed before responding, her blue eyes wide. "Hello, Mother." She bent down and picked up Marilou, cuddling her close.

Adele let her eyes flicker to the doll for a moment.

"Is ... is Marilou's dress torn?" Just like a man to let something like that happen without fixing it.

"Yes, Mother." Judy resumed her seat and began brushing her doll's hair with her fingers, rocking her gently.

Adele understood that. Sometimes when she was small, she would comfort her dolls when she most needed reassurance. "Perhaps I could fix it."

Judy wrinkled her nose and hugged Marilou even closer. "Perhaps."

"I'm sure I could."

Her eyes pinioned Adele so hard that she wiggled under her daughter's gaze. "Aren't you busy?"

"No, not too busy to fix her dress."

"But you have better things to do."

"Maybe I don't anymore. Maybe I've cleared my schedule and come down to see you. Maybe I'm not ever going to be too busy for you again." Adele glanced at Troy but found his face immoveable. He wasn't going to offer her any help. She almost wished he would interfere for once. Make her path easier.

She took a hesitant step toward Judy. "Darling, I wish ... I wish you'd look at me."

Judy glanced up then back to her doll. "Why?"

"Because ... Judy, you know that I love you, don't you?"

She frowned, set her doll on the ground, and stood up. Looking her mother in the eyes, she said, "I don't."

216

"Well ... I *do* love you. You must believe me, darling, I do." *I'm ruining this. I've got to show her somehow.* "Judy, I didn't know I did either, you see, until you left, and then I realized that ... that ... that everything is dreadfully empty without you. There's not much reason for living if I don't have my little girl about, helping me at the shop or making me breakfast or ... or any number of other things."

"I burn the toast," Judy said quietly, "and I put too much sugar in the tea."

An odd detail, but she could reassure Judy there. "I like my toast burnt and my tea sugared."

"No, you don't! You're always angry 'cause you don't!" Judy snapped. "And I guess you won't have me around to burn your toast and sugar your tea anymore!" And with that, Judy dropped to the floor, buried her head in her arms, and began crying.

This shocked Adele. Judy never cried, and 'never' could be taken quite literally. Even as a tiny baby she had been quiet, almost resigned, as if knowing that unnecessary noise was more likely to bring disgust than comfort. As she grew, she would become even quieter when she was hurt or sad. But now Judy was crying, and Adele didn't know what to do with herself.

"Judy ..." she began several times, but words wouldn't come. Troy was still impassive; he offered her no help. So she dropped down next to Judy and gathered her into her arms.

"I just don't know why you hate me. I try so hard

..." Judy whimpered, burying her face in her mother's shoulder.

"I don't hate you. I don't."

"Yes, you do! You don't like me. You wish I'd never been born. I'm never good enough for you."

"Of course you are!"

"No, I'm not. I never can get that toast out in time … I don't know if I ever will!"

"Forget the toast, Judy; it doesn't matter. I'll make the toast," Adele whispered, smoothing Judy's hair back from her face.

She kissed her forehead and tucked it under her chin. She wasn't sure what else to say. Not sure how to communicate things she'd never been able to speak before.

"But I *want* to make the toast! You never make it crisp."

"Then Daddy can make your toast."

"But you want to take me back to London! I don't want to go back to London … I want to stay here. I like it here, Mother, I like it here."

Adele swallowed "Then you don't have to go. I'm not going to make you go anywhere you don't want to go or do anything you don't want to do. I promise, Judy. And if you'd rather stay with Daddy, that's okay. I won't try to take you away."

The girl shifted and sniffled. "You won't?"

"No."

Judy wiped her eyes, mostly on the front of

Adele's dress. "You're sure?"

"I'm very sure."

"But then I won't see you again," Judy said.

Adele's heart stopped for a moment. Her daughter wanted her. Her daughter would be sad if she couldn't see her again! She breathed out softly and forced herself to address the matter at hand.

"I can come here to visit, and you can come visit me sometime. We'll figure it out, Judy. Don't worry about it."

"But won't I have to go to boarding school?" Judy asked in a very small voice.

Adele winced. It was apparent her daughter was quite apprehensive of that former plan of hers ... though she wasn't quite sure how she knew about it. Had Millie told her? She was the only one other than Hal who'd known.

"No, darling. I'm not sure how you heard of that, but I won't send you to boarding school. Hal wanted me to, and I thought it was a good idea at first." Adele sighed. "But I broke up with Hal, Judy. So I could keep you."

Judy cocked her head. "So you're not marrying Hal?"

"I'm not." Adele shook her head emphatically. "I'm through with him. He wasn't right for us, Judy. He wanted me to give you up ... and that is something I won't do. Never again. I promise."

Judy breathed an audible sigh of relief. "Good. I

didn't like him very much."

Adele smiled weakly. "I can see why. He didn't pay you much attention, baby. But that's all right." She hugged Judy close again. "I like you a lot more than I like him. So, after this summer, you'll come home to me, and we'll start over, all right?"

Judy nodded slowly. "Yes. But ... but I don't think it'll be the same. I'll miss Daddy a lot, you know. I wish you could stay here."

Adele couldn't resist a brief glance at her ex-husband, whose face was expressionless save for a dash of curiosity. "Oh, baby, I can't," she whispered.

"No, Judy's right, Adele." Troy cleared his throat as Adele and Judy turned at his voice. He met Adele's eyes evenly. "It *would* be difficult to arrange for you to spend time with Judy. I don't think you'd better come visit. I think you'd better live here."

Adele swallowed, blinked twice, and finally processed his words. "Excuse me?"

"Live here with Judy and me. It makes sense. You can't forever be running from London to France and back again. But if you stayed here all the time, it'd cut down traveling expenses. It makes sense to me." He shrugged and leaned an arm against the door frame. "What do you think?"

"Yes, Mother, please stay!"

"What ... what are you saying, Troy?" Adele stuttered. She was the nervous one now. She was the one who could scarcely handle the beating of her heart, the trembling of her hands.

She felt she was going to faint, but she didn't—simply awaited his answer.

"I'm saying I want you here. Living without you is almost as hard as living with you. *Almost*." He flashed a teasing grin before it dropped, and his gaze never wavered; his voice wasn't trembling now. "If you're ready to start being Judy's mother ... Della, don't you think you should be my wife?"

The Lady of the Vineyard

Chapter Eighteen

Judy had been tucked into bed, more exhausted than she was willing to let on but unable to resist sleep, and Holt locked in the house to avoid distractions. The sun was still setting over the sea in brilliant golds and pinks set above and about the deeper blue of the sea and the greens of the vineyard. Adele had forgotten how beautiful it was here, a perfect garden paradise.

How had she ever considered this her prison? Had she not the strength, the resources, to thrive in such an environment? Yet she had thought that when she was newlywed, and within a few months, she had succumbed to boredom and bitterness.

The Lady of the Vineyard

Perhaps she had already been unhappy before she married Troy, though. The thought was a fragile one, but she was willing to allow it some hold in her soul. It was true, wasn't it? It hadn't been Troy's fault she had been a miserably unhappy young woman. Even Adele wasn't insane enough to blame him for that.

At first, she and Troy walked between the rows of half-ripened grapes in silence, then he asked a stupid question about her health, and she responded and asked about his. After that, the conversation flowed naturally enough. Not as well as she'd have liked, but then, there were too many walls between them now for complete honesty, and too much history for complete comfort.

"Do you remember this?" he asked, as they had arrived at one of her favorite spots to sit, overlooking the sea and the sprawling vineyards and the little town tucked to the west.

Of course. That was something she'd never forget, if she lived to be a hundred. "Mmhmm. It's still a beautiful view. One of the best in the world. Shall we sit?" Perhaps if they didn't have the excuse of movement, they might move past small talk and begin to be helpful. There was so much to discuss, most of which she hadn't allowed herself to think about. Even now, her mind struggled to catch up. She only half-believed his offer was serious, and even if it were serious, she was fairly certain it was a poor idea.

She wanted to believe him, though. Even in the

face of the idiocy that renewing their ghost of a marriage would be, she wanted to believe that a man like Troy Kee could have a steadfast love for her that could fill all those empty places she kept finding in her soul. Yet that couldn't be true. No, Troy hadn't been able to do it before, and he couldn't, even now, with added maturity. Adele certainly couldn't be everything for him. She didn't have it in her nature to be a good influence. How lonely Troy would be, the only one with any worth within him in the marriage.

Yet she sat, and Troy next to her, both stiff and on complete opposite ends of what felt like too small a bench for the both of them. She remained silent, eyes glued on the horizon, and waited.

"I suppose I should start since this is my scheme." He cleared his throat. "I will be honest and say I deeply care about you. I really can't stop. And I'm sorry about that, because it would be easier for us both if we could slip into a convenience situation. Affection would be easier in this case, or a kind of friendship. But I admit I love you, and as such, I wouldn't be happy with half a marriage. So in asking you to stay, I'm asking you for everything. I'm not sure I have much to give in return, but then, neither do you."

At least he was honest about that now. Adele had nothing left to give. "You know there have been other men since ..." She winced. "Not Hal, actually, but other men."

He stiffened but his expression stayed the same. "I

thought so. I hoped not, but I didn't expect anything else, and I can't bring myself to judge you for it. When I look at life from your perspective, there's no reason why you shouldn't have."

"Do you mind?" Perhaps that was the deal-breaker. After all, he was a particularly sanctimonious chap at times despite the fact that he'd married her, knowing her beliefs—or rather her lack of beliefs. He was a mixed-up man, or at least, he had been.

"Honestly, yes, but could our relationship be any more torn up? In my ... my religion, I suppose you'd say, it constitutes adultery, but all of this is rather messy. There is no option here that completely satisfies my need for a tidy, moral life." He turned slightly, and she was forced to meet those blue eyes again. Was it any wonder she'd fallen for him once? "But that's my fault as much if not more than it is yours. I was the idiot here. I thought, all those years ago, that I would marry you and change you. Instead, you changed me, and brought out all the lies I told myself, and forced me to face the man I really was—which is exactly what anyone with a brain in their head would have told me, but I wouldn't have listened. I don't think I was much of a Christian at all until a few years ago. Oh, I believed it was all true, but that's nothing. It wasn't anything but a set of facts to me and a vague idea of how I ought to act. It wasn't until you left me that I realized I had nothing to comfort me—no faith, no hope, no love. So, after the divorce was finalized and all the little details resolved, the busywork over and my mental collapse finally allowed free reign, I disintegrated."

"Oh." Was that what had become of him for six whole years? "I assumed you wanted nothing to do with us, but were you—?"

"I was being stupid." He grinned and looked back over the sea. "Harrington kept the vineyard going, and I drank excessively, slept little, drove my car recklessly—to the point where Harrington feared I had suicidal intentions and took away the keys. I knew if I tried to contact you in the slightest, you would take one look at me and file for full custody. So I bided my time—a selfish impulse, but it preserved Judy." He shuddered and lowered his eyes. "I couldn't have borne for her to see me like that. She deserves a lot more than the man I was. But, slowly and steadily, with Harrington's help, I picked myself back up. After I was sober and shaved and sleeping regularly, God managed to get through to me—which was funny, because you always hear about such conversions happening when you are at your lowest. But I suppose without Harrington, I could have gone lower still, and the fact is, I believe God was working behind the scenes. He knew I was in no state to be reasoned with, and I believe there is a lot of reason to Christianity." He smirked, that funny little sideways grin. "Anyway, since then, my life has taken a dramatic upturn. Harrington reminded me this year that I've now been delaying the inevitable, which is involvement in my child's life, for too long. I'm not likely to drink too much or drive too fast or anything similar again—God's got me tied up too tight this time. There's no wiggle room."

"I'm glad you're happy ... or, you know, that you found the thing that you want to believe in." She felt her cheeks heat, as that had sounded entirely wrong. What she wanted to communicate was that, since religion was an actual comfort to him rather than a burden or a type of torture, she was glad Troy had found his way back to it. "Do you know what I mean?"

He chuckled and shook his head. "I've an idea. You're at times the most pleasant atheist I've ever known, you know? And at times such a little horror."

"Thanks," she mumbled drolly.

"Oh, don't mention it. But here's what I did want to say, as we ought to be clear. When I married you the first time, it was an upfront to the commands of my God. I'm not supposed to marry a non-Christian. But over the past few days, God had spoken to me quite a few times, through Scripture and through reminders of His nature. He's been reminding me of the grace He possesses—and He's been telling me that He's willing to consider us married if we are."

Adele smothered a laugh. "If that's a line, so help me, Troy—!"

"It's not a line! It's an honest to goodness thought." He smiled then grew more serious, taking her hands and squeezing them. "Look, I just want you to know how I'm viewing this. God forms our lives around living, breathing people, and I know He has a plan regardless of my stupidity. What I'm hearing from God is, if you're absolutely willing and believe you would like to commit to a relationship, until one or the other of us dies, for Judy's sake—which I grant is a big stretch—we could remarry, legally, but spiritually, this is more of a healing relationship than a new one."

"So basically, you want it to be as if we were never divorced?" Even Adele was skeptical of that. "That honestly feels ..." What was the term her mother used? "Extrabiblical if not unbiblical."

He cocked his head. "That was surprisingly well-put for someone who doesn't know or care about such things—as you have often said. Yes, I know it's a stretch. I'd want to talk it over with a few more people, too. However, I feel very convicted about that. I don't know if you've heard people toss that word—*convicted*—around as much as I have, so maybe it sounds silly and shallow to you by now. But for me, in this one situation, it suddenly doesn't feel silly and shallow. It feels real and true and of the moment."

"I see." Though she truly didn't. Wasn't he just finding a way to justify his feelings for her? Adele had done that herself so many times—the thought process was familiar. Yet Troy's eyes held all the simple sincerity they always had.

"The truth is, I believe God's grace extends even past, at times, the rules that govern relationships. Not exclusively, but though I believe at one point or another remarriage was forbidden—" He hesitated then shook his head. "Lola mentioned the verse to me, but I can't remember it, and I suppose you wouldn't care. That said, I don't feel God would prohibit us from remarrying. Again, contingent upon your promise of forever."

"What if I can't make that promise?" Adele wanted to, but it seemed like a poor choice. Most of the best things in life were transient. She believed in the concept of marriage until death; however, reality had always shown it to be impossible.

"That's why it's a contingency. I can't have you running at the first sight of trouble. I need you to stay with me for Judy. Then, when she is grown and gone, if we are not deeply in love again, as I dearly hope we may be, we can at least be good friends. I think, after another twelve years or so have passed, we probably will be."

Her lips twitched with suppressed mirth. "What makes you think that?" There was no evidence behind such a statement.

"Because I like you, really, even when I hate you, and I think you feel much the same. Besides, there's so much to be done here, and of course when Judy is grown, we can still take an interest in her—in her education, and her career, and in any future family she made choose to start, et cetera. I want to be friends with Judy until I die, too. I'm not asking you to love me, but to commit to living with me." That smirk appeared again, this time accompanied by an odd little twist. "And if I can do anything to make you fall in love with me, I will do it, too. I think I can put up a better fight now than I did before. I can't make you love me, but I can make it hard not to."

With this, the laughter bubbling below the surface, both a bit hysterical and a bit genuine, burst forth. It took her a few minutes to recover completely, though she felt his eyes on her the whole time. "Your confidence astounds me. Haven't I broken you yet?"

He shook his head. "No, and I don't intend to let you. You're going to be third in my life from now on, by necessity. God first, then Judy, then you. With God first, I'm not afraid of any more breaking—and you'd have to understand that this would be a life lived for Judy until she's grown, and then ... well, then we get to decide what our relationship looks like, but I know for sure that I won't put you before God again, so I feel safe in that way."

How nice for him. If only Adele had that same assurance. "I wish I had something like that, for I am afraid of the breaking process. I know I may seem cold, but I grieved our marriage, and I grieved for Judy, and I pretended not to feel it. I could only blame you for so long before, at last, I had to see that it wasn't your fault. I've at last come to the place of being unable to hate anyone but myself."

"I suppose that's an improvement." He stood and reached a hand out to her. "Yet hating yourself is also a form of selfishness, of focusing on you instead of others, so I'd rather you didn't do that either."

She took his hand and rose. "That's an interesting way of putting it."

"I speak from experience. Let's head back before it gets dark and cold."

"It's never cold here this time of year," Adele protested, but she still let him lead her back to the path. As the dimness of the early evening, followed by a pleasant breeze, set in, they ambled back through the vineyard rows, again in silence.

He stopped just as they came in sight of the house. "Just think about it. If you're willing to commit to the remainder of your life with me, I would like us to remarry and live here. As long as we can, at any rate—I know things in Europe are insecure, but this is my home, and I want it to be Judy's—and yours. As I mentioned, I don't think I would be able to manage a chaste marriage. Well, really there's no such thing, but I wouldn't want to invent a new category of matrimony."

"Neither would I." Love was one thing, but lust ... Adele could manage that. Crude, perhaps, but it was reality. She wasn't going to marry him without certain benefits. That was, *if* she chose to marry him. "I'll need some time to consider this."

"Of course. There's no rush. I'm leaving you my room and sleeping with Harrington, though if you find me on the sofa tomorrow, that's because I got thrown out. He's not a great friend."

"Right." She withdrew her hand from his. She'd hardly realized he had held onto it. "I'll see you tomorrow, then."

Troy reached up and rubbed the back of his neck, and she thought she caught a glow on his cheek she hadn't seen before. "See you at breakfast ... if you deign to show your face, I mean." If that glow had been a blush, he managed to control his voice enough to not let on to his bashfulness.

"Of course I'll be up. I've got to make sure you're not putting any more strange ideas into Judy's head." She smiled and turned, leaving him behind as she scurried up to the house ahead of him.

In his room, she turned on the lamp on the desk and found her suitcase had already been placed on the bed. She opened the latches, but her eyes caught on a frame on the bedside table.

Leaving the suitcase where it was, she picked up the framed photograph of herself, seven years younger and laughing. Her old self seemed so youthful, so different from the Adele Collier of today. Funny how habitual Troy had removed the picture of his own family—his parents, himself, and Lola as a tiny baby—and put her in this important place. A quick glance confirmed that that old photograph, grainy and unfocused, rested on the desk now.

She oughtn't to snoop. She oughtn't to. But curious if his habits remained the same, she opened the top drawer of the bedside table.

Everything was much the same. Handkerchiefs, a journal of sorts in which he kept random thoughts—a record of things he wanted to remember—cough drops, and a scattering of snapshots, both in an album and loose. Yes, he was still a creature of habit.

Some of the snapshots were new, though. There was one of Holt, for whatever reason, and then a collection of baby photos of Judy. When had he taken those? They were clearly done by him, not a professional. She reached in and collected a few—wrinkled, well-loved things. The only thing she'd left him of the child they created together.

Guilt swarmed in her stomach like a hoard of locusts. She dropped the photographs back in the drawer and took out his journal. Though that might be an invasion of his privacy, well, he had always let her look at them before.

He'd been working at this particular journal since 1931 according to the date on the inner cover. She flipped toward the end and found a few entries from the last few months.

"Dishes tomorrow—down to last cup."

"Carrots, parsley, broth."

"Harrington present, book, something by that Christie woman."

"Bring two hats to London."

"Get Judy new shoes, lighter, for walking."

"Get Judy's doll a bathing suit, if such a thing is to be found."

"Take Judy to see a play some time."

The Judy-related entries continued for some time, and that made Adele smile. He had so many ideas for things they could do together, for things he thought she needed. This reminded her of the single-minded devotion he had shown her in the early days of their marriage. How she'd appreciated that attention—even going so far as to believe he could heal all the holes in her heart with that love.

Yet Troy didn't believe such a thing was possible. Perhaps it was better to expect less. It meant you always received more.

At last, she replaced the journal and, with a sigh, undressed and slipped into her pajamas. There would be time to worry about that in the morning.

The Lady of the Vineyard

Chapter Nineteen

The conversation was long and included so many different considerations that Troy was unsure if they could ever hope to conclude things. They sat for hours in the parlor at the front of the house, her on the sofa and him at his desk, sitting backwards on the chair. He rocked it back and forth in the silences that ensued as one of them had to think through a tougher question.

Yet he had hope, for Adele was much-changed. She spoke gently of Judy, a mother's heart emerging for the first time, and he was excited about that.

It led to a greater boldness in him, to the point where he even asked if she would consider having another child. Adele said she would, perhaps, but he would have to be heavily involved in the process. She reminded him that he'd never quite raised a baby–and though she admitted that Millie had taken a large part in raising Judy, at least Adele had observed the process from the beginning to the age of six. That was something.

Troy admitted to needing some education, but he felt, especially if they were to have a baby at a time when his work schedule wasn't as heavy, he might be able to help Adele.

"Especially," he added, "if we weren't fighting. I believe that was our principle problem when it came to Judy's early days. We couldn't stop quarreling. And I don't intend to fight. I intend to admit we have, at times, irreparable differences in our beliefs and in the way we see things, and I intend to move forward under that assumption. I'm not going in blind. I know exactly who you are, and I hope you have a good idea who I am."

"I think I do." She cocked her head. "I also think I was in a darker place during those months than I have been willing to admit up to now. However, now that I know, and now that I have grown up a bit, I think I'd be less likely to fall into such a malaise."

They talked about this, too, at some length. Adele stumbled over her words whenever her father and brothers were brought up, and therefore, Troy tried to get her to talk more about them.

She wouldn't, but he thought he understood better. She had grieved them deeply, and more than that, her mother's grief and the leftover scars of what seemed to be a largely dysfunctional family had plainly left their mark on Adele. She spoke affectionately of her brother Kenneth, especially, and repeated her desire to have a little boy someday. Troy wondered if that were an entirely healthy impulse. He wasn't going to press at her wounds any more than he had to in order to stimulate healing, but it seemed she was eternally looking to replace something that had long been lost. Either that or ignoring the loss. Neither were healthy.

Yet he loved her. He told her that, many times, and rejoiced in the telling. It made her less uncomfortable as he said it more often, and she started to laugh about it, to push back, to demand 'why?' He had no proper answer, only an emotional one, which he knew would not be good enough for her. Yet it would have to be, for it was all he had to offer.

Eventually, they circled back to religion, as they often seemed to anymore. "I've started taking Judy to church, which is in French–I really ought to think about taking her to an English-speaking church, especially if ... well, if you stay."

"Judy will likely be able to learn French, though, at her age." Adele leaned back on the sofa and drummed her fingers on the arm. "I doubt it'll be much of a problem with her, as it was for me."

"She'll learn, yes. That's why I've been taking her,

actually–I want her to speak it before she must go to school. But I want you to attend church with us."

"Oh." She cocked her head and stared at him in silence for a full minute before she spoke again. "I suppose I could attend. I'm not usually welcome in churches, though. I mean, they take one look at me and …"

He'd heard that story, actually. "Honestly, what you're wearing now would be fine, Della. No one's going to judge you. I'm sure of it."

Her brow furrowed, and he knew she wanted to believe that. He could see the struggle in her brown eyes, the struggle to accept the possibility that she might be accepted somewhere–as the person she was.

"I could come along, as long as people are kind," she said at last. "I don't think I'd get much out of it, but I'd agree to come, so Judy has that structure. I suppose, if I were to structure an ideal life for a young child, it would include some sort of structured community, like a church. I'd hope it would be less … well, less traditional than the one I grew up in."

He thought what Adele associated with tradition was truly a judgmental atmosphere. He couldn't fault her for that, even though he hoped eventually he could make her associations toward organized religion more pleasant. He didn't dare to hope that she would eventually come to abandon the idea of religion entirely in favor of a more personal relationship with a Savior. Yet Troy could never give up telling her about that.

240

After they had exhausted all available subjects, Troy and Adele called Judy into the parlor. Her eyes were wide, and she went to sit on Troy's lap.

"Is Mother going to stay?" She blurted out the words, then flushed.

He squeezed her shoulders. "Yes, we think so. We know that's what you want, but we still have some decisions to make. Your mother needs to see what it would look like to sell her shop, or at least rent it out, and there's Aunt Millie to think about—and your Granny, of course."

Judy nodded, glancing between them. "But then Mother will live here?"

"Yes." Troy smiled over Judy's head at Adele. "That's what we've arrived at, after much discussion."

"So what's next?"

"Well ..." Adele stood and walked to the window. "I suppose I ought to go back to England and sort things out. I'm not sure what remarriage entails ... Is it more complicated than being married the first time?"

Troy shook his head. "I don't think so, but I'll look into it."

"Mm ..." She fingered the curtains. "These are coming down, too."

He glanced at Judy. "I suppose remodeling is our first priority."

"Not first, but sooner rather than later. It's something to do at least." Her hand dropped, and she sighed. "There's a lot of work to be done, Troy. A terrible lot of work, if we have any hope of making a life. It's frightening, but I suppose if we take it one step at a time ..."

"I don't believe it'll be as difficult as we've made it out to be." Troy rose, setting Judy to the side. "At least, I don't think so. We've talked and talked about all the potential problems, all the things we'll have to work on, and yet there are so many blessings to be considered. If only because of Judy ..." Again, he looked at his daughter. She was like him–willing to hope again and again.

Oh, God, let this time be a hope that is anything but shattered.

"Yes." She turned from the window and stepped back around the room, touching things lightly, a trace of judgment at times evident as she examined his decoration. Frankly, it was good to have her back. Troy knew what the parlor looked like; he just wasn't sure how to fix it. "I'm sure we can make a great deal of life. It'll take a few months to get things arranged, but after that—"

"After that, we can just do our best to face each new day with new determination." He put his hand on Judy's shoulder. "Our baby can teach us a lot about that. She's nothing if not faithful."

"Oh, don't put that pressure on her. She'll grow up thinking she can make the difference in our relationship. Which she can't. You know that, don't you, Judy? Daddy and I aren't fighting about you—we never are. If we're foolish, it's not about you."

"It'll take a lot more showing and a lot less telling to convince her of that, Della." Troy had never had to live through the fighting of parents, but he'd read some about it, and he understood the basics. It could be quite harmful to a child, if any of these modern-day psychologists were to be trusted.

"I know, but we can start by telling her, and then not fight in front of her. That was part of the plan, wasn't it?" She raised her eyebrows.

Troy bit back a snapping remark and simply nodded. "Yes. I've a feeling I ought to have gotten that in writing, though."

Adele rolled her eyes at him and walked over to his desk. "I'm going to call Millie—and then my mother. They'll want to know what we're doing."

As Adele picked up the telephone, Troy sat down on the sofa and pulled Judy into his lap.

"It's going to be all right, I guess?" she whispered. "You're going to make it all right for us, Daddy?"

"I'll do everything I can, baby." He pressed a kiss to her cheek. "But just you wait. God can do so much more than I ever could. Trust Him—and pray like crazy, baby."

Adele cupped her hand over the receiver. "You'll need a lot more than prayer, Troy. But I am determined."

"And who dares stand in the way of a determined Adele Collier—er, Adele Kee?" Yet even so, he knew

Adele was wrong. It would take a lot of prayer, and for him, a great deal of time spent in Bible-reading, to get them through this. It would be a mighty battle, and God would have to win the war for them.

But if faith could move mountains, he wasn't too worried about it helping Adele and him find their way together.

Chapter Twenty

They left for London a few days later. Millie was thrilled, of course, and Mother seemed similarly thrilled—if a bit skeptical. Adele had an idea that it might be a while before Mrs. Collier adjusted to the idea of the remarriage.

Yet this was what she wanted, wasn't it?

Adele shook off that thought whenever it popped up. Her resolutions seemed like decisions made by another woman. How had she even got to that point?

As she sat in her kitchen, Judy and Troy in her bedroom and Millie sitting across the table from her, her mind began to wander. There were so many things that could go wrong. She believed in Troy's determination; her own was questionable. She didn't trust herself. Yet if she didn't follow through, Judy's heart would be broken—and she couldn't bear to break her daughter's heart. No, she'd do anything to prevent that.

"I can see you spiraling." Across the table from her, Millie stirred sugar into her tea, a small smile coloring her lips. "This is the right decision, though. You know I'm right or else you never would've made it in the first place. Just trust your instinct—and please consider opening your heart to thoughts of God again. It'll make things so much easier."

Adele refrained from an eye roll. Those hurt Millie, and if she was going to reform in one area, she might as well try to reform in the others. Yet she couldn't resist a sigh. "I know, Millie. I know. I've promised Troy to attend church with him and Judy, but I doubt I'll go further than the performatives. Still, Troy wants Judy to be raised a Christian." Whatever that even entailed. It hadn't been an easy road for Adele.

Millie took a sip of her tea. "Mm-hmm. And what about the actual wedding?"

"It won't be much of one." Same as last time, they'd have a simple legal ceremony at the register's office. This time, however, Mother would be present— along with Millie, Troy's sister and her husband, and of course Judy. "We'll probably go to my mother's house for dinner afterwards, though, which will be uncomfortable."

"I admit your mother can make even the most simple occasion formal, but surely she's thrilled about you getting remarried." Millie adjusted her glasses and flickered her eyes about the kitchen. "On a lighter note, I suppose you'll give up the flower shop."

"Yes, if you don't mind. I say we rent it out—and if you like, your place over it. That ought to be enough to cover the rent for this flat. Then you could take it!"

Millie's brow furrowed. "But half of that money should be yours."

"I don't need it! That way you can put something away with your own salary." Adele shrugged. It seemed like the perfect solution to her. "Troy assures me we'll do well enough that I don't have to worry overly much about money as long as I'm cautious. He's worked hard at his vineyard, and with investments, and I think we'll be okay."

"If you're sure. But once we finally sell that place, we'll sort out the financials accordingly." With a decided jerk of her head, she returned to her tea.

Adele smiled into her own cup. Millie's organized soul needed to get everything settled before she could bask in the probable joy Adele's return to her husband had likely caused.

"Troy says as soon as Judy has re-outfitted Marilou, we can—oh, there you two are."

Troy ducked out of the bedroom, Judy right behind him lugging her large doll. "She has a variety of outfits, so we had to try a few looks. Like all women, Marilou is fussy about her outfits."

Judy frowned. "It was for a wedding, Daddy, so we had to think about it a lot."

He reached behind and ruffled her hair, smiling, and his voice had a roll of a laugh to it. "I know, baby, and I wouldn't have it any other way." His eyes lifted to Adele then. "Are you ready to go? Millie can come if you like."

"But I won't. I'd rather get a few things settled here." Millie rose. "I'll see you all after dinner."

After Millie left, Adele slipped her shoes back on, and the three left her flat behind. Judy chattered incessantly with Troy making occasional comments, yet Adele remained silent. She watched them, reminding herself again and again that this was the right thing— and that Judy deserved more than just a mother, especially when the mother in question was Adele.

They walked to Lola and Dave Cole's house, and as they walked, Adele's dread gerw. What would she say to Lola? She'd avoided speaking with her as much as possible, going as far as to avoid letting her visit Judy to keep from having to look the woman in the eye. She knew Lola Cole was aware Adele had broken her dear and only brother's heart; she further knew that it was a trespass not easily forgiven.

How much she feel now? Lola might seem more flighty than Troy, but she had a strong mind, and she held firmly to her convictions. More so than Troy, she would hold onto a grudge.

Yet Adele must face her, and must admit that she had been in the wrong, and must beg, perhaps even without speaking, for that forgiveness. It wasn't necessary, granted; Troy had made his decision without consulting his sister, and he always would. However, Adele knew how miserable the rest of her life would be if she couldn't get Lola on her side, or at least on the side of maintaining unity.

Yet Lola's smile was wide when she opened the door and ushered them into her little townhouse. The Coles had done well for themselves—Adele knew Dave had worked his way up through a bank in London, but she hadn't realized it had led to this type of wealth. She supposed they also had no children to worry about, and had started young, and knowing the couple, likely worked hard. Still, she was impressed by the simple but elegant home. There were so few people doing well these days. The war and then the economy had wrecked the lives of so many.

Troy and Lola talked about arrangements while Adele stood toward the back of the group, for once glad not to be the center of attention. Eventually, they were ushered into the living area and told to take seats— except Adele.

"Adele, could you come to the kitchen and help me? Oh, no, Judy, why don't you sit and chat with your daddy and Uncle Dave? That's right, baby."

Unable to resist the call, Adele followed Lola to

the back of the house to a small kitchen, probably converted in recent years from some kind of butler's pantry.

"You know I don't need help." Lola crossed to the stove and checked on a pot then turned to face Adele. "But I needed to talk to you, and I thought this the most convenient way, which you probably surmised."

Adele nodded. She'd known from the beginning that she'd be called to task. The question had only been how quickly Lola would manage it.

Apparently, quite quickly.

"This is a sudden change. Of course, you realize this, but that makes it no-less sudden. I'm sure you know that Dave and I wonder what prompted such a change—and that there has been some discussion as to its sincerity."

Adele blew a breath between her tight lips. "I can understand why you would feel that way. I would assure you that I am genuine in my desire to renew my marriage, and that I am doing it all out of love for Judy, but I know my word has not meant much to you before. Why should it not?"

Lola cocked her head. "So you understand my position. You must also understand that I love my brother dearly, and that save for Dave, he is all I have in the world. I saw you crush him before. I don't know if you understand this, but you thoroughly destroyed him, and I feared ... Well, I feared he would take his life. To see him go through that again would be torture, and again, I would fear the same. Especially now that Judy is more than a baby. She would have always felt the sting of missing him, but now ..." She shrugged. "I can't see her coming back from that. I want her to be happy, and I want Troy to be happy."

"That's what I want, too." More so Judy than Troy, but she cared about Troy, too. She didn't want to hurt him again. Especially since that would invariably hurt Judy.

"Good. The other thing worth mentioning here is that God has things under control. I must believe this is as much part of His plan as all the rest, even if it's hard for me to see that." She pulled back a chair at the kitchen table and gestured to another one across from it.

Adele took the seat. "I won't pretend I have the same beliefs, but I do feel this is for the best."

"Mm." Lola lowered herself across from Adele, rested her arms, one decorated with two silver bracelets, on the table, and pinched her lips together. "I know Troy's decision has been made and is final, but if I had any sway with him, I won't be shy in admitting that I would encourage him to think twice. You're not a Christian, and the Bible clearly states that being 'unequally yoked,' as we call it, is forbidden. Yet Troy seems to have found a way around it, and he insists God has given him permission to move forward. And, after all, it is his life and his choice."

"You just don't agree that it is a good choice."

Adele tilted her head. "I quite agree. On the surface, it doesn't look like a good choice." Her heart shuddered at the words, but it was true. "I have hurt Troy immeasurably, and Judy even more so. Judy is the innocent in this, and we want to do right by her. Perhaps it would've made more sense for us to come up with an arrangement for her to spend equal time with both of us. Instead, we chose a patch-up that may look foolish and certainly will not be easy."

"I quite agree!" Lola lifted her hands as if in surrender, her bracelets jingling together. "Yet Troy loves you. Do you realize what a gift that is?"

Adele nodded. "More and more, I do. It will make things easier."

"That, and he doesn't love easily. It's an honor. I hope you don't take it lightly. Not this time." Like Troy, Lola's eyes were capable of holding a hard glint when they needed to.

"No, I won't."

Could she keep that promise, though?

The door flew open, and Judy burst in. "Mother, Aunt Lola! Daddy's teaching me French. But did you know? Uncle Dave knows a lot of French, too, and now Daddy's mad."

Lola's eyes immediately let go of Adele's. "Uncle Dave shouldn't have let on that I've taught him some. Well, sweetling, let's go pacify the poor little man."

Adele had to shake her head at Lola referring to Troy as 'a little man,' but it was easy enough to be derogatory toward one's brother; a husband was quite another thing. Which he would soon be to her once again.

Heavens, her life was spiraling out of control—or into order? Which was it?

Adele and Lola rose and started back toward the front of the house. Halfway there, Lola paused and pulled Adele into a hug. Surprised, Adele didn't manage to react until Lola had already drawn back, holding her by the arms, and given her a light shake.

"I'm happy to have you back in the family, despite all my fearsome warnings. It'll be nice to have a sister."

Then she turned and scurried toward her husband and brother, leaving Adele in shock.

The Lady of the Vineyard

Chapter Twenty-One

They were man and wife again.

She sat beside him at the dinner table, but he over-focused on Judy in an attempt to avoid worrying.

He knew all the risks now. He could predict everything that might go wrong—he knew his faults, and he knew hers. This was a much riskier game ... or at least, now he knew all the rules.

Yet that was an old perspective from the days when it had been a game. A terrible game with no winners, a cruel game, but a game no less.

Now it wasn't a game. It was a relationship, and one which Troy was determined to not fixate upon. God came first, then Judy, then Adele. That was the way it had to be, even if everything in him screamed that his relationship with Adele ought to secondary—not last.

Yet if they had any hope of making this work, especially since she was not a Christian, it needed to be about Judy. Adele said that, over and over again, as if repeating it would make it true.

Yet he knew now what marriage was supposed to be, and their relationship could only be a shallow imitation. Unless she became a Christian.

Troy thought she might. He didn't think God would allow him to renew their marriage if He didn't have a long-term plan that included Adele's salvation. But Troy couldn't make that happen—he could only pray and witness to her in any way he could.

Perhaps that was his problem. He needed to have faith. It wasn't 'only' prayer. Prayer was a powerful tool, after all. God would hear him—and show him how to act in every moment of this new life.

Again, he focused his thoughts back on Judy, but he allowed the comforting thought to sink in. God was with him—and with his family. His plans would prevail, even despite Troy's human idiocy.

At last, the dinner was over, and Judy was sent off with Millie for the night—and Troy and Adele were left to wander back to her flat alone.

They lingered in the streets, taking a walk to a nearby park where he'd fed birds with Judy not so long ago—oh, but it felt like a lifetime. She talked lightly about this and that, not showing a hint of the nerves that would've made his hands tremble if he hadn't kept them clenched in fists.

Finally, he got the nerve to ask a question that'd been bothering him all day: "Are we going to do the whole wedding night thing this evening or am I a couch husband for the time being?"

Her eyebrows arched. So that'd been a stupid question. Good to know. "I thought you made it clear you weren't a couch husband."

"I'm not, but I would understand it if you wanted to put it off."

"As if 'it' were so repugnant that I'll fake a headache every chance I get." She clucked her tongue. "I thought you knew me a little better than that."

Thank God. "I just wasn't sure—"

"You worry too much."

He had a lot to worry about, but she was still right. "Right. 'Heaviness in the heart of man maketh it stoop: but a good word maketh it glad.' That's Proverbs."

"Mm." No resistance and no agreement. That would probably be how it was at first, but perhaps it'd eventually break through to her heart. He'd keep quoting what he knew—and learn more. That'd be a good project to take on with Judy; she was so hungry for truth.

However, he wasn't much worried about Judy tonight. "Should we head back?"

Adele scoffed. "Men."

Troy had to laugh at that. "Not just that. It's

getting dark. Besides, why on earth would you want to delay?"

She smiled but didn't reply. They turned back in the direction from whence they'd come nonetheless. He liked feeling her hand in his once more, small and soft and cool. Adele didn't have comforting hands—the word he would've used was inciting. Yet in another way, holding her hand did soothe him. He was slowly letting himself admit just how much he'd missed her.

When they arrived back at her flat, she started fussing, which she'd expected. Adele hated being placed in a corner, even one of her own choosing. So he sat at the table and had some toast and watched her fuss.

She's regretting it. She's already regretting your marriage, and she's going to leave you. Pull back before you're too attached.

Yet he shook the thoughts free and focused on praying.

He cleared his throat. "What about children?"

"Didn't we already talk about that?"

Yes, but not in the context of immediacy. They'd talked about having another child eventually, if things were working out, but Troy didn't believe she'd be exactly thrilled if she ended up pregnant in the first month.

Though how likely was that, really? Surely the same thing wouldn't happen twice. Besides, they were older now. Not that old, but perhaps they wouldn't have their second child that quickly, even if they did leave it up to chance.

He shrugged. "I meant ... what about tonight?"

"We don't need to worry about it for at least another week. And I'm willing to take the risk. If it happens easily, of course I'll have one more baby with you, as promised." She slid into the seat across from him. "I admit I'm nervous about what that'd look like. Can you imagine us raising a second child? But I'll have you this time, which will make a difference—and Judy, of course."

"Right. You'll have me." Perhaps it was enough that she knew he'd be there—and that she intended to rely on him. "Besides, you love Judy. Surely you would love another child just as much." At least, he hoped so. He wanted to believe so.

"I would, of course, but I'm not sure it would come on as quickly. I know more about what the commitment of having a child is like." She shrugged, her eyes beginning their restless wandering about the small kitchen once more. "I fear my own behavior as much as anything—and I know that my love of Judy comes because of who she is, not because she's my child."

"I don't think that's entirely true. I can't imagine you attaching yourself to a little girl who wasn't your own." She was everything but maternal; however, her devotion to Judy proved her mothering instincts weren't as absent as she claimed. He saw something in the way Adele had looked at their daughter in the last few weeks that gave him hope.

Hope was as risky as it was vital.

"'Hope thou in the Lord,'" he repeated under his breath.

"Hmm?"

"Oh, it's a Bible verse. Psalm 42 ... I can't remember exactly what verse. 'Why art thou cast down, O my soul? and why art thou disquieted within me? Hope thou in God: for I shall yet praise Him, who is the health of my countenance, and my God.'" He smiled. "I was actually trying to get Judy to memorize that one."

Her brown eyes returned to his face then. "You know I don't believe a word of it. Actually, when I hear that kind of thing, I think, 'How ancient.' The wording of the Bible has always made it seem otherworldly and historical. How can it possibly be relevant? How is it any different than memorizing some inspiring poetry?"

Hmm. So she does have thoughts beside disinterest. "I suppose it's not that different if you aren't a Christian. However, to me, at least, I believe it's the literal word of God, which rather changes my perspective about its objective truth and usefulness."

Her head moved slowly up and down, chewing on her bottom lip. "I see. As I said, you're welcome to do whatever you want with Judy. I hope you intend for her to live in a version of the real world, at least, though."

What was more real than the Christian life? He wondered what she felt was idealistic about his beliefs. There was definitely a lot more to explore on that front—and her curiosity more often than not gave him hope.

There was a lot to be hoped for. Yes, there was. Though the future was uncertain, God's peace filled him as he watched her fidget across from him.

They could start over. They could, and they would.

The Lady of the Vineyard

Chapter Twenty-Two

Adele closed her eyes and leaned back against her arms folded behind her head. She relished the sunshine beating down on her face, arms, and legs. The sunshine was marvelous, and she was glad of it on occasion, despite the fact that sometimes it burned too hot for her taste in France.

However, now it was lovely, and she enjoyed lying there, listening to the sea gently shush against the sand, the seagulls cry, and Judy and Troy laughing as they played in the surf. The lazy August day had afforded a perfect rest for the insanity of the last few months, and she was grateful for the escape.

Long ago, she'd put aside the novel she'd been

reading and taken to relaxing. Her wedding ring dug into the back of her head, and she shifted her hand to accommodate it. Yet she was adjusting, once again, to the cold band and the solitaire diamond that bound her to the man playing in the surf below. It was more about her commitment to Judy than Troy, truly, but she admitted her loyalty to the man was starting to arise. Particularly, as he was a good lover; secondarily, as he was a caring and faithful man.

Thankfully, though, the days of her being spoiled were long past. It wasn't good for her, and anyway, it was no foundation for a healthy relationship. Instead, Troy asked her, with both his actions and his words, to take part in spoiling Judy. At least, for the rest of the summer, that was something Adele could readily agree to. School would show Judy, soon enough, that she was not nearly as special as her parents were currently treating her. At least, that was her opinion. Troy seemed to believe that he'd be able to rein himself in and properly discipline Judy eventually. Adele rather doubted it.

At last she sat up, hearing them come running toward her, and pushed the hat back from her face.

"Having fun?" she asked.

Troy grinned and set Judy on the picnic blanket beside her. "Loads of fun! Working up a healthy appetite for that picnic lunch." He bent down and kissed her neck. "Among other things."

Adele pushed him away. "Oh, go on. Sit down."

She'd forgotten during those years how things were between them—but she had the idea that Troy would never let her forget again. But it was nice that some part of their relationship was fully functional and delightfully fun. Even if it was the only part. *Yet*. There was time to discover the rest.

Judy scooted up next to Adele. "What do we have?"

"Just sandwiches. There are some biscuits, but you have to have some vegetables first. Or at least—here, have an apple."

Judy wrinkled her nose. "I have to?"

"Yes, you have to. And so does your father."

Troy gasped and fell back against the sand. "Cruel woman!"

"Oh, shush, Troy." Adele opened the picnic basket. "Cruel indeed! I'm trying to make both of you be at least decently healthy. Honestly, I don't know why you don't weigh a thousand pounds, the way you eat."

"I just don't worry about my weight; it takes care of itself." He grinned. "I'm a grown man; I don't have to eat healthily if I don't want to."

Adele narrowed her eyes but softened her expression with a smile. "You'd better if you know what's good for you, Troy Kee."

Troy fake growled. "Vegetables make my nose grow."

Judy's eyes widened. "Oh, Mother, if vegetables make his nose grow—"

The Lady of the Vineyard

"No! Both of you settle down and do as I said." Adele had to take some form of authority over the situation, or she was going to go mad. She wasn't going to let them squalor in their unhealthiness a moment longer.

Judy's diet had been a wreck when she arrived there two months ago, and they were only starting to settle down now that they'd taken care of the legalities of being remarried and moving in together. She was able to take them in hand now, and she was determined to do so.

After all, that was being a mother, wasn't it? Bothering her family about eating healthily? She assumed so. She'd never seen a healthy, full family before, outside of Millie's, and even then, it was through a window. Not being a participant rather limited one's views.

After eating, Adele insisted they pack up and go home. She had some research to do on the schools here, and she wanted to finish it that afternoon. That was another thing she felt sure a mother would do.

As they drove home, Adele laid out some of her plans for a garden behind the house, and Judy fell asleep in the back seat. Glancing over his shoulder, Troy told Adele to cover her with his coat.

"I've got something to say to you, too. Something important."

Adele paused in her arranging of the jacket and sat leaning towards him in the front seat. "What is it,

Troy?"

"I would hold off with the schools and the gardening. We might end up in England in a few months. It's becoming a serious possibility, anyway."

Adele's nose wrinkled. "What do you mean?"

"I mean I think France is going to be at war with Germany, one way or the other, and I think we'd better prepare for that possibility." Troy's hands were gripping the steering wheel tight now. "We will probably be in England in that case. I can't have my family in a war zone."

Adele swallowed. She didn't want to be in a war zone, either.

"I think the most important thing in the world is that we're together, though," Troy said. "I can't be grateful enough for that, come what may."

Adele nodded. She wasn't able to say she was grateful yet. There had been good things about being back with her ex-husband, a family again—and bad things. The bad things mostly came from her own restlessness, her guilt, her disappointment—and the fact that she wasn't exactly in love with her husband.

She still hadn't been able to fake love. Not as well as she would have liked.

Perhaps some day she'd be able to pretend she was in love with Troy, enough so that she'd convince him and even herself, but she wasn't too convinced she'd be able to.

However, it was nice to be with him despite her

emotional apathy. She liked him a lot, she'd come to realize, and she somehow knew that, despite it all, she was doing the right thing.

"I'm grateful, too," she said at last. She let her hand slide across the seat until it almost touched his leg. He glanced down, the corner of his mouth quirked up, and he took her hand in his.

"I'm glad of that." He squeezed her hand and caught her eye for a moment before returning his gaze to the road. "I love you, you know."

She leaned her head against his shoulder and closed her eyes as the car began the climb up the road to their home. "I know."

Perhaps, for now, that would be enough.

To Be Continued …

The Kees & Colliers series will continue with book 3, *Flowers in Her Heart*.

A Note to the Reader

Welcome to the section of the book that I cannot guarantee you read. I always read any kind of material the author writes at the end of the book, though, so I decided I would write it anyways.

I pray this novel blessed you, but if it didn't, no worries. Post a review either way!

This book is one I wrote directly after finishing my first-ever novel (which is part of a completely different series, The Chronicles of Alice and Ivy). I never expected it to become a series (it ended up being book 2 after some revisions), nor did I expect it to be longer than a short story.

However, here I am, with this full-length novel being published.

The idea for this story originally bloomed out of *The Parent Trap* and *GiGi*. Basically, I wanted to play with the idea of a divorced couple and the complicated situation their separation left behind for their child.

Obviously, it has expanded a lot since then. However, you may remember, if you have followed me since the beginning of my author journey, that several different editions of this novel have been out. The first version ever was launched in September 2016—so many years ago!

Though so many things have changed about the novel, the core story has remained the same: an exploration of family, of second chances, of sacrificing selfishness for the sake of those you love. Adele was heavily inspired by the arc of the main characters in *The Bird in the Tree* by Elizabeth Goudge, an excellent and under-appreciated novel.

God bless you & keep you—may He make His face shine upon you—may the Lord lift up His countenance upon You and give You peace.

Kellyn Roth
April 2022
White Salmon, WA